# Cornish Folk Tales

## for Children

Mike O'Connor

Illustrated by
Michelle O'Connor

The History Press

*My grandchildren:*
*Charlie and Ellie Pearson.*
*The best proofreaders ever!*

First published 2018

The History Press
The Mill, Brimscombe Port
Stroud, Gloucestershire, GL5 2QG
www.thehistorypress.co.uk

British Library Cataloguing in Publication Data.
A catalogue record for this book is available from the British Library.

ISBN 978 0 7509 8449 2

Typesetting and origination by The History Press
Printed and bound in Great Britain by TJ Books Ltd, Padstow, Cornwall

# Contents

Adro dhe'n Awtour ha Lymnores

# About the Author and Illustrator

MIKE O'CONNOR OBE is an expert in folklore and ancient music from his home of Cornwall. He is known for his work for the TV series *Poldark*: selecting and arranging the historical music and writing lovely songs for Demelza. Among folklorists he is known as a great storyteller and for his research of the world of travelling storytellers in Cornwall, a world described in his best-selling *Cornish Folk Tales* and revisited in this book.

Mike is a storyteller, fiddler, and singer, as is Anthony James, one of this book's heroes. Sometimes writer and character are hard to separate!

MICHELLE O'CONNOR, Mike's daughter, is an artist and art teacher. She too is deeply engaged in traditional arts: dancing, singing, and playing the violin.

She understands the stories and their Cornish landscape intimately. She knows that sometimes the stories seem to grow from the land of their birth, and that is reflected in her atmospheric illustrations.

In creating this book it's as if father and daughter are travelling the lanes of Cornwall together, in the footsteps of Anthony and Jamie, swapping stories, writing and sketching as the miles and words flow past.

Aswonvosow

# Acknowledgements

I thank Maga Kernow for Cornish language advice, Michelle for her great illustrations, my fellow storytellers for their inspiration and encouragement, the storytellers of old for keeping the culture alive, and Anthony James, for taking us all on wonderful journeys and always bringing us safely home.

*(Mike)*

Raglavar

# Introduction

This book tells some of the best folk tales from Cornwall. Also, it is the story of Anthony James, a travelling storyteller. Anthony was born about 1767 in Cury, on the Lizard. He learned the fiddle as a lad, and could play at dances and sing to entertain. Britain was then at war with France and Anthony served overseas in the army, but in the last years of the century he lost his sight and was repatriated. A military pensioner, he was accommodated in Stoke Military Hospital, Devonport in the Winter, but in Spring he crossed the Tamar to earn a living.

Anthony was known as a 'droll teller'. In Cornish dialect a 'droll' is a story, delivered in speech, rhyme, song, or any combination.

The word's origin is the Cornish word 'drolla', meaning folk tale. Guided by his son, Jamie, Anthony walked the Duchy in the late eighteenth and early nineteenth centuries, living on tales, songs and tunes.

Like Anthony, most of the 'supporting cast' are also real, though I have changed a few dates.

Cornwall is a special land with a unique culture. Once independent, it has its own classical literature, music and its own Celtic language. Though in decline, the Cornish language was then still spoken in the far West, especially by fishermen and smugglers …

Anthony is fondly remembered as being from times past. But his stories and songs live on. So, let us start our journey. Once again let us travel through Cornwall with Anthony James.

To help us on the road each chapter has a riddle associated with it. The answer is usually at the end of each chapter.

In many places we would begin 'once upon a time'. But this is Cornwall, so 'En termyn eus passyes …'

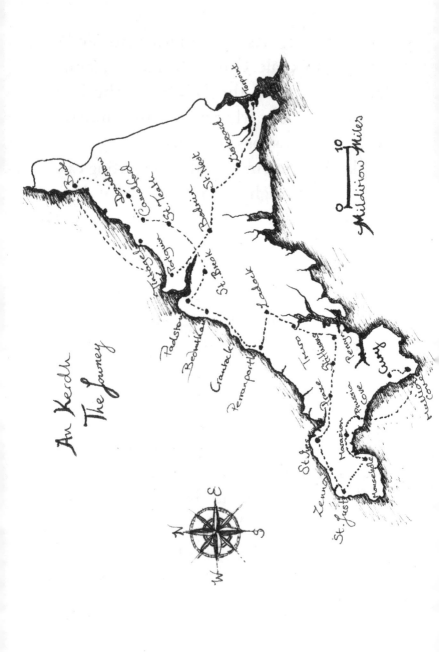

An Kerdh
The Journey

Mildinow Miles

Bude
Dungastow
Camelford
St. Teath
Tintagel
Portquin
Bodmin
St. Neot
Liskeard
Torpoint
Padstow
St. Breok
Bedruthan
Ladock
Crantock
Perranporth
Truro
Gilliang
Perry
Cury
St. Buryan
Rose
Russia Cove
Hallow Cove
Zennor
Marazion
St. Just
Mousehole

# 1

## ONAN

# Torpoint: The Droll Teller's Son

*In my bed I never sleep,*
*I often run but never walk,*
*Slow and wide or fast and steep,*
*I often murmur, never talk.*

Beside the great river it was very dark. Young Jamie had been there all night, waiting and watching. He could hear the lapping of the water; it was nearly high tide. Then he heard oars splashing and voices in the darkness.

Then the first light etched the hills. He could see the outline of the ferry. In the bow was a tall figure. Jamie's heart raced. He had waited for this moment for a long time.

'Dad!' he shouted. The tall figure waved.

The ferryman moored the boat then helped the tall man ashore. The tall man offered money but the ferryman laughed and shook his head.

'No sir,' he said. 'Your tale paid the fare. I haven't laughed so much for ages.'

The tall man held a stick which he swept from side to side as he stepped forwards.

'Jamie!' he called. The boy ran to him and gave him a great big hug.

Jamie was a bright lad, but he had never been to school. In those days only the children of rich people went to school.

Jamie lived in the village of Cury in West Cornwall. His mum taught him to count: 'onan, dew, tri, peswar, pymp*', and to say the Lord's Prayer: 'Agan Tas nei, eus yn nev* …'. People there spoke Cornish as much as English.

Importantly he learned the words 'En termyn eus passyes' which is like 'Once upon a time'. This was because Jamie's dad, Anthony James, was a storyteller. Blinded in the wars with the French, in Winter he lived in Plymouth in a military hospital.

But now it was Summer. Jamie had made his way to the River Tamar to meet his dad. For when the days were warm Anthony James went round Cornwall telling stories, playing his fiddle and singing songs. He was a travelling droll teller and young Jamie was his guide.

Each had a pack on his back and each carried a fiddle. In their heads was a world of stories, songs and tunes. Together they began walking across Cornwall.

Where the going was good Anthony would walk unaided, tapping his stick against the kerb or wall. Where the road was rough Anthony would place a hand on Jamie's shoulder. But now, such was their joy at being together, that though the road was good they held hands tightly.

Then Anthony spoke. 'Jamie, it's 75 miles from Cury to Torpoint. How did you do it?'

Jamie laughed, 'Two days ago I walked towards Helston. I met Mr Sandys from

in their heads was a world of stories, songs and tunes

Carwythennack. He asked a carter and got me a ride to Falmouth. There I met Frosty Foss the droll teller. His cousin drives the mail coach and I travelled with him. I sang songs all the way. In Bodmin I found Billy Hicks in Honey Street. He let me sleep by his fire. Next morning he gave me porridge. Then he spoke to another coachman so I got another ride. I saw Bill Chubb when they changed horses in Liskeard – he waved to me.'

'Jamie,' smiled Anthony, 'you are a wonder.'

Then as they walked they swapped jokes, riddles and tall tales: the very best way to make the miles fly past.

*(A river)*

---

\* onan, dew, tri, peswar, pymp – counting one to five in cornish.

\* agan tas nei, eus yn nev – 'our Father, who art in heaven…'

# 2

# DEW

# Cotehele: The Hunting of Edgcumbe

*Every day, I never move,*
*I never change my stance.*
*I go from Launceston to Liskeard,*
*But never Plymouth to Penzance.*

'This is Edgcumbe country,' said Anthony. 'The Earl of Mount Edgcumbe that is. South is his mansion: Mount Edgcumbe. Up river is his house of Cotehele.'

'The Earl knew about Robin Hood. Do you remember when Robin hid underwater in a river and breathed through a reed?'

## *The Hunting of Edgcumbe*

Richard Edgcumbe of Cotehele and Henry Trenowth of Bodrugan were deadly enemies.

One day Bodrugan brought his soldiers to capture Richard. They nearly took him by surprise. But Richard heard the hue and cry at Cotehele gatehouse. He was outnumbered so he fled through the servants' quarters, out of the back door and into the kitchen garden, chased by Bodrugan's men.

Richard hid among the trees above the River Tamar, but then he was spotted. The only way he could go was down towards the river. He said, 'If I escape I'll find a way to thank God.'

It seemed that Richard must either fight or drown. But he was outnumbered ten to one. Then he remembered Robin Hood. He waded into the river, throwing his cap into the stream where it would be seen by Henry's men. Then he plucked a reed and hid under the water, breathing through the reed like a straw.

his hat was floating in the middle of the river

Bodrugan looked everywhere for Richard, then he saw that his hat was floating in the middle of the river. He thought Richard had drowned.

Richard hid until Bodrugan's men left. Then at night a boatman rowed him down the River Tamar to Saltash and from there he escaped to Brittany. Eventually he had his revenge on Bodrugan, but that is another story.

In Cotehele woods beside the River Tamar, where Richard Edgcumbe outwitted his pursuers, there is a chapel built by Richard to give thanks for his escape. It's dedicated to Saint George and Thomas à Beckett, but everyone just calls it the 'Chapel in the Woods'.

*(A road)*

# 3
## TREI

# Mount Edgcumbe: The Lady and the Sexton

*Little Nancy Etticoat*
*In a white petticoat,*
*And a red nose.*
*The longer she stands*
*The shorter she grows.*

George Edgcumbe's parties were the very best; everyone looked forward to them.

George was the Earl of Mount Edgcumbe and in 1761 he married a charming young lady called Emma, daughter of the Archbishop of York.

So that year all their family gathered for a very special Christmas party at their house of Cotehele. But on Christmas morning, when the Earl came down to breakfast, there was no sign of his wife. 'Strange,' he thought, for she was an early riser. A maid was sent to the Lady's room. She returned, weeping, 'I think Lady Emma's dead.'

George rushed upstairs. His wife lay in bed, deathly pale. The doctor came. He said there was no sign of life. George was very sad. On his wife's finger was the beautiful engagement ring he had given her just a few months before.

The body of Lady Emma was put in a coffin and loaded onto a boat. With muffled oars it was rowed down the River Tamar to Mount Edgcumbe. Solemnly a hearse carried it to Maker Church. Everyone watched as it was placed in the Edgcumbe vault. There was the Earl, the servants, the coachmen, the boatmen, the vicar, the churchwardens and even the sexton (the church's caretaker).

They then went home, all very sad at the loss of this beautiful young lady. All that is, but one. The sexton ate his supper that night with a grim smile on his face.

As soon as it was dark he took a candle lantern and a sharp knife and returned to the church. Silently he entered the Edgcumbe vault and put the lantern on a handy tomb. He prised open the coffin and raised the lid. There was the body of Lady Emma. Her skin was deathly white. A rose had been placed at her throat, and her hands were crossed on her chest. On her left hand was the diamond ring. It sparkled in the candlelight.

The sexton tugged the ring. It would not move. He tugged again. Still it did not move. So he took his knife and placed it against the ring finger. He held the blade against the flesh. He pressed harder.

'AAARGH!' he screamed, as Lady Emma sat bolt upright in the coffin and looked straight towards him. Abandoning his lantern he fled, screaming, into the night. Later he was found in Millbrook village, babbling wildly.

That evening the Earl dined alone at Mount Edgcumbe House. He had forgotten all about Christmas and parties. As he ate he looked from the window. He saw an eerie light approaching through the trees. As it drew closer he saw a pale female form in a funeral shroud, carrying a candle lantern, walking straight towards him. He recognised his own wife; he thought it was a ghost.

He was filled with horror as she approached the house. He heard the door open, so he ran upstairs. He heard steps on the stairs, so he hid under the covers of his bed. He heard the bedroom door open and lay shivering in terror. Then he felt the cover being drawn back and he opened his eyes to see a bloodstained hand. Then he heard his wife's voice. 'I'm so cold,' she said. 'Husband, you must warm me.'

Trembling with fear, he reached out to hold the ghost. To his surprise he found it was real, and not a ghost at all. Food and drink were brought. The small cut on Lady Emma's finger was bandaged. The doctor was sent for; he said she must have been in a trance. The Lady and her Earl returned to Cotehele for the best Christmas party ever and lived happily for many years.

The ghost of Lady Emma was never seen again because it never really existed. But sometimes, if you go to Maker Church on a dark night, you can see the shadowy figure of a sexton fleeing across the fields, certain he has just woken the dead.

*(A candle)*

# 4

## PAJAR

# Liskeard: Bat Rowe's Bear

*Sometimes short,*
*Sometimes tall,*
*Sometimes true,*
*Or not at all.*

It was a weary road to Liskeard. But when they arrived Anthony and Jamie cheered up. At the Barley Sheaf pub was their friend Bill Chubb. He said in all his life he'd only ever been to two places: Truro and India! After supper Bill smiled mischievously and began to speak.

## Bat Rowe's Bear

I'm goin' to tell 'ee about a Liskeard man called 'Bat' Rowe: a bad-tempered chap. Right niffy he was! He hated foreigners: people from Bodmin or Plymouth. 'Furriners' he called them. This was unfortunate because Bat Rowe ran a lodging house at the bottom of Higher Lux Street. As most of his customers were 'furriners' he was grumpy most of the time.

His rates were cheap because the building was old, the furniture rickety and the rooms small, so it was favoured by itinerant workers, players, droll tellers and the like.

In those days France was having a revolution. It was not safe for travelling people. So two Frenchmen, Jacques and Pierre, came to Cornwall to earn a living in a friendly place.

They escaped from France in a Cornish fishing boat. The skipper, an experienced smuggler, avoided both French and British naval patrols. He secretly brought the travellers to Looe Quay in the dead of night, when the Exciseman was fast asleep*.

No one saw Jacques and Pierre scramble ashore and set off towards Liskeard. On the road they saw no one. In Liskeard they asked for the cheapest place to stay and, of course, they were directed to Bat Rowe's boarding house.

They asked Bat if he had a room free. He nodded. Yes, he had a small room left. He didn't like letting a room to someone from Plymouth, let alone Paris, but trade was trade, and he needed the money.

'Give me the five shillings now,' said Bat, 'I have important business tonight in the Barley Sheaf. Now listen, I don't want you coming in late. I've had enough of finding inebriated foreign bodies on my doorstep.'

Then Bat took the money and left.

At this point I can reveal that Jacques and Pierre had a secret. There was a third member of their party. It was big, furry, and strong, and even more grumpy than Bat Rowe.

'Excellent,' thought Jacques and Pierre as they paid Bat Rowe the five shillings. 'With Bat out of the way we will be able to smuggle our dancing bear into the room without being seen.'

After supper Jacques and Pierre got the bear from the copse where it was hidden. They led it into town along side roads and back alleys so no one would see them.

But when they got into the boarding house they found that the door to their room was so narrow they couldn't get the bear in. They pushed and pulled but whatever they did, the bear was bigger than the door. Eventually they gave up and went to bed, leaving the bear, who by now was rather hungry, in the dark corridor outside.

Late at night, Bat came home from the Barley Sheaf. It had been a demanding meeting and he was rather worse for wear. He was too mean to light a candle, so he felt his way along the corridor until his foot connected with something soft and resilient on the floor.

'I bet it's those furriners,' grumbled Bat. He gave the body on the floor a kick and shouted out, 'Take your boots off and go to bed!'

Now the object of Bat's attentions was not used to such treatment or such bad language.

...and the shape he kicked got up and ROARED !!!

Understandably angry, the shape he kicked stood on its hind legs and roared. Bat heard the unexpected sound, lit a match and was horrified to see a hungry and bad-tempered bear advancing towards him.

Bat Rowe shot out the door as fast as his legs could carry him. Like a champion sprinter he ran back to the Barley Sheaf, where he knew the town Constable was chatting to his friend the Exciseman from Looe.

Hearing the noise Jacques and Pierre got up and placated their furry friend. They decided to go to Bodmin where, they had been told, the bear could pass as a local. They gave the bear a pasty for breakfast and quietly led it into the night.

When Bat returned ten minutes later with the Constable and the Exciseman there was no sign of the bear or the Frenchmen. In Looe no one had seen the little boat arrive at the quay. No one had seen Jacques and Pierre clambering ashore or walking to Liskeard. In Liskeard no one else had seen the bear.

'How much have you had to drink?' the Constable asked Bat Rowe.

Ever since then, in Liskeard, when anyone makes an unbelievable suggestion, the response is usually, 'Ah, just like Bat Rowe's bear!'

*(A story)*

* Excisemen were stationed in sea ports to collect taxes.

# 5

## PEMP

# St Neot, the Stags and Crows' Pound

*My fingers point to far away,*
*My head points to the sky.*
*I help the traveller every day,*
*But all men pass me by.*

Jamie was sitting under the signpost at the crossroads on Goonzion Downs, eating a Cornish pasty. A crow landed close by: it was skinny, with ragged feathers. It was so sorry-looking that Jamie threw it a piece of his pasty. The crow ate it as if he were starving.

'Thank you,' said the crow.

'You're welcome,' said Jamie, without thinking.

'Do you know what this place is?' asked the crow.

'No,' said Jamie, beginning to realise how unusual it was to meet a talking crow.

'I could tell you,' said the crow, 'especially if I had another piece of pasty.'

'How do I know that you won't just eat the pasty and fly away?'

The crow looked affronted and raised its beak into the air. 'I am not a jackdaw,' it said. 'I'll have you know, my cousin the chough is really King Arthur in disguise.'

Impressed, Jamie threw it some more pasty.

'You are at Crows' Pound,' said the crow. 'It was built by St Neot.'

## St Neot and the Stags

Neot was a holy man with magic powers. He was only four feet tall, but that didn't matter. He could command the animals and the birds. He founded an abbey on the edge of Bodmin Moor. He was so famous that even King Alfred came to visit him.

But one dark night thieves stole the oxen from the abbey farm just when they were needed for ploughing. Neot asked the animals of the forest to help and two stags came and pulled the plough for him. Each night Neot thanked the stags for their hard work and let them go back to the forest. Each morning the stags returned.

The thieves were amazed. They gave the oxen back and never stole anything again. From that day each stag had a white ring round its neck where they had been harnessed to the plough. These stags led a charmed life, free from hunters and blessed with plenty of food.

'Neot sounds a nice man,' said Jamie.

Then the crow continued.

## The Crows' Pound

On the edge of the moor there was never much food for crows. Then when the farmers came they pulled up the wild plants that gave us seeds and berries and planted wheat and barley instead. So, when their backs were turned, we ate just a little of their grain to make up for what we had lost.

But then the farmers invented scarecrows, and used boys with catapults to scare us away. We crows got hungrier and hungrier.

Then Neot came. He told the farmers that on Sunday they should leave the fields and go to church. For a whole day the fields were unguarded. At last the starving crows could fill their empty bellies. The crows looked forward to Sundays, the one day of the week they would not be hungry.

But then the farmers were angry. They sowed the fields again and they guarded them every day. The poor crows and their chicks were starving and Neot was not happy either, for no one went to church.

When Neot asked why no one was in church, the farmers said it was the crows' fault.

'Why?' asked Neot.

'The crows eat the corn. Without it we cannot make flour. Without flour we can't make bread. Without bread our children will starve.'

Neot was sad to hear this and he said he would find a way to stop the crows robbing the fields whilst the farmers were in church.

At the top of Tripp Hill, Neot made a square field with a hedge of moor-stone and turf. When he told everyone it was a pound for crows, they laughed at him.

'The crows will just fly over the wall,' they said. But they did not laugh for long.

On Sunday Neot rang his bell. His magic made every crow for miles around come to the pound. When everyone heard the crows were in the pound they went to church.

In the pound the crows found lots of fuzzy bushes, with bright yellow flowers and seeds to eat. And, being musical birds, they joined in with the hymns in the church.

Since then, from seed time to harvest, the crows are sent to the pound every Sunday. On other days they find food wherever they can.

'Sometimes,' said the crow, 'we earn a crust telling stories to travellers at the roadside.'

'Crow,' said Jamie, 'we are birds of a feather,' and gave him the rest of his pasty.

*(A signpost)*

# 6

# Bodmin: The Monks of Laon

*A horse's tail,*
*Teases string,*
*Stick dances,*
*Trees sing.*

In Bodmin they rested outside St Petroc's Church.

'Where will we sleep tonight?' asked Jamie.

'In a hole in the wall,' said Anthony.

That did not sound comfortable. Jamie was about to complain when a jolly man arrived. It was Billy Hicks, the Bodmin storyteller.

'Anthony,' he said, 'did you hear about the fight?'

'No,' said Anthony, looking surprised.

'Surely you heard about the fight!' said Billy. 'It was right here, in August!'

'I never heard of a fight in August,' said Anthony.

'Yes,' said Billy, 'August 1113!'

Anthony spluttered, then said, 'Billy, I bet you started it!'

They all laughed. Then Billy said, 'Actually it was King Arthur's fault!'

## The Monks of Laon

Arthur is famous here. Many Cornish places are named after people in his stories. Tredrustan: Tristan's house, Tremodret: Mordred's house, Kea: Sir Kay, Treator: the home of Arthur.

In 1112 there was an uprising in Picardy in France. On Maundy Thursday the cathedral of Laon was burned down and the unpopular Bishop Gaudry was murdered, despite hiding in a barrel in his palace.

To rebuild the cathedral, a group of nine canons* took the Shrine of Our Lady of Laon and some relics on a fundraising tour of France and England. The relics caused miracles, like healing the sick, and these were offered in return for donations.

In the Summer of 1113, as the canons rode from Exeter to Bodmin, they were told they were in the 'Land of King Arthur' and were shown places like 'Arthur's Chair' and 'Arthur's Oven'.

At Bodmin they were welcomed by a friendly prior called Algardus. They set up their shrine and began their fundraising.

A blind girl was made to see again. A deaf boy had his hearing restored. But then came a man with a withered arm, hoping to be healed.

A Frenchman called Haganel asked him about King Arthur. The Cornishman said that Arthur was not dead, but just asleep, waiting to be called should his people need him.

Haganel burst out laughing and said he was a fool for believing such a thing. But the people of Bodmin were outraged that

their man was being insulted. With sticks and staves and pruning hooks they chased Haganel three times round the churchyard and then into the church.

They only stopped when Prior Algardus appeared brandishing his crozier. He sent everyone home, which was harder for the Frenchmen than for the Cornishmen!

This all happened long before Arthur is mentioned in the history books.

Then Billy led them to an inn called The Hole in the Wall. They played their fiddles for their supper and were allowed to sleep in the stable.

*(A violin or fiddle)*

*canon – a senior priest.

*crozier – a holy staff.

# 7

## SEYTH

# Port Quin: The Watcher of the West

*Never thirsty,*
*Alive without breath,*
*Never dry,*
*Cold as death.*

Next day Anthony and Jamie followed a winding track beside the River Camel. Anthony wanted to cross the river at Wadebridge, but the bridge and quays were guarded by soldiers. Frustrated, they continued through St Minver to the little harbour of Port Quin.

There everyone was talking about a French privateer*, the *Black Prince*, that had been sinking Cornish fishing boats.

Mr Knill, the Exciseman at St Ives, had seen it heading north.

'That might explain the soldiers,' said Anthony.

That night Anthony and Jamie slept in a shed full of fishing nets.

The following morning they breakfasted on fish. Then to Jamie's surprise they were led to a fishing boat. The skipper's name was Tommy.

'He's a rascal,' said Anthony, 'but he's a good sailor.'

They set sail. Anthony said, 'I like the wind on my face. We should be in Padstow soon.'

'As long as we round Pentire before the tide turns,' said Tommy.

Jamie looked at the rocky headland ahead of them. Suddenly he called out. 'Dad, I can see a Giant!'

'I'll tell you about him,' said Anthony.

---

* privateer – a private ship licensed to attack enemy vessels.

## *The Watcher of the West*

Once there was a careless Giant. He didn't have a proper job and he trampled cornfields and flattened cottages by mistake. People got fed up with this so they went to Tintagel to ask King Arthur to help.

Arthur sent Sir Kay, one of his best knights. But Sir Kay returned with his armour dented and his sword bent. 'He's too big,' said Sir Kay, 'I couldn't even scratch him.'

Then Arthur sent Merlin the Magician. But he returned with his wizard's hat dented and his wand bent. 'He has so little brain,' said Merlin, 'magic doesn't work.'

'This is tricky,' replied Arthur, 'but don't worry, I'll think of something.'

Because the people trusted Arthur they began to boast about what they would do once the Giant had been defeated.

'We will make him our slave.'

'We will bind him with chains.'

'He will work for us night and day.'

But the wind carried these foolish boasts to the Giant. He was very angry and trampled fields and cottages deliberately, so the people suffered badly for their boasting.

But at Tintagel there was a young squire called Amouraine. He wanted to become a knight, so he rode out to try and defeat the Giant.

When he got to St Minver he felt the earth tremble as the Giant's feet thumped the ground. Amouraine's horse bolted. Amouraine was thrown off and his arm was broken. The Giant picked him up.

'Are you the Giant?' asked Amouraine.

The Giant scratched his head and thought. 'Um, yes,' he replied. 'Who are you?'

'I am Amouraine.'

'What do you want?' asked the Giant.

'I want to fight you,' said Amouraine.

The Giant burst out laughing. 'You are brave, but very silly. I hope you're not one of those who want to make me a slave.'

'Yes,' said the squire.

'So you are my enemy,' said the Giant.

'Yes,' said the squire.

'What a pity, I might hurt you!' was the reply. The Giant was about to toss the boy into the sea when he saw that his arm was broken. He put him down. 'Go,' he said. 'I do not fight injured men. That would not be fair.'

When Amouraine got back to Tintagel he told Arthur what had happened.

'The boy is a fool!' said Sir Kay. 'Punish him!'

'No,' said Arthur, 'he was brave, so I shall make him a knight. Also, he has shown me how to defeat the Giant.'

Next morning, before anyone was awake, Arthur left Tintagel. He had no armour, no sword and no horse. At St Minver he felt the earth tremble.

'Who are you?' asked the Giant.

'I am Arthur,' answered the King.

'Arthur!' cried the Giant. 'You are my enemy!'

'You kill my people,' said Arthur, 'and that cannot be!'

'Your people would enslave me,' said the Giant, 'and that cannot be!'

'Then,' said Arthur, 'let us settle our quarrel in a fair fight.'

The Giant studied Arthur. 'Where is your horse?' he asked.

'I thought you might hurt him.'

'Where is your armour?'

'It's no use against you; it's foolish to waste it.'

'Where is your sword?'

'You would break it like a twig. It's a shame to break a good sword.'

'You are at my mercy!' laughed the Giant.

Arthur smiled.

'But this isn't a fair fight,' said the Giant. 'What shall we do?'

Arthur said, 'Instead of fighting, let's talk. I heard that you would not fight Amouraine because he was injured. I know you will not fight an unarmed man. I think at heart you must be good, even though you trample fields and cottages.'

'But your people want to make me a slave,' said the Giant.

'I won't let them,' replied Arthur. 'Instead, I will give you an honourable task. While I live

eyes fixed on the far horizon

you shall guard this land, watching the seas for approaching enemies. When I leave, then you shall watch for my return.'

So it was agreed. At last the Giant had a proper job. The people of Cornwall were delighted. 'Proper job!' they said, and they still do.

That was long ago. For centuries the Giant has sat by the sea. The wind and the spray have darkened his skin so it looks like rock, and the grass has crept up his motionless limbs.

He still waits there, quiet as a statue, his eyes fixed on the far horizon, gazing across the stormy water, waiting, watching, longing for that dawn when King Arthur will return.

We call him the Watcher of the West.

*(Fish)*

# Tintagel: Arthur's Birth, The Sword in the Stone, Excalibur

*Silver coinage carved in light,*
*A penny none can earn.*
*I sleep by day and walk by night,*
*And watch the seasons turn.*

Around the headland appeared a two-masted vessel flying a French flag. Tommy looked through his telescope. 'The *Black Prince*!' he said. 'Bear away, bear away!'

As the little fishing boat turned to the north-east, Jamie heard a bang and a cannonball splashed in the water behind them.

Tommy growled, 'Drog yw*! If they hit us we'll be scat* to pieces.'

The French privateer was catching them fast. But then there were more bangs. Around the headland came two British ships. Through the telescope Jamie read the names: *Phoenix* and *Shaftsbury*.

'Just in time,' said Tommy. 'Those Frenchies were so busy looking at us they never saw who was coming up behind!'

The British privateers were firing at the *Black Prince*, which turned towards Padstow. The ships sailed out of sight as the battle continued in the Padstow Estuary.

Tommy spoke: 'Padstow's not for us. We don't want to get caught in a sea battle! Anyway, the tide's turned, we're going north, like it or not.'

Ahead was a rocky island.

* drog yw – means 'it's bad' in Cornish.

* scat – a word meaning broken (literally 'scattered').

## *Arthur's Birth*

'That's Tintagel,' said Anthony, 'where Arthur was born. His mother was Queen Igraine of Cornwall. His father was Uther Pendragon, the high king of Britain. That meant Arthur was heir to the throne of Britain.

'Merlin knew that many rivals would want to kill Arthur, so he secretly smuggled him out of Tintagel. He took Arthur to a far-away castle. There he was raised by a trusted knight called Sir Ector, as if he were his own son.

But no one told Arthur that he was heir to the throne; that was kept a secret too.'

### The Sword in the Stone

Now Sir Ector already had a son called Kay, who was older than Arthur.

One New Year's Day Kay went to a tournament but forgot his sword. Arthur was acting as his squire, so Kay sent him to find another sword.

Outside a great church Arthur found a sword stuck in a stone. On the stone were the words: 'Who pulls the sword out of this stone is the rightful king of England.'

Arthur held the sword and pulled. It slid from the stone as if from butter.

Arthur took the sword and gave it to Kay for the tournament. But then Kay took it to his father, saying, 'Surely I must be king.'

But remember, Ector knew the secret about Arthur. He made Kay tell the truth and Kay owned up that it was Arthur that got the sword. Then Merlin announced who Arthur really was.

Many tried, but no one else in all the land could pull the sword from the stone, so at the feast of Pentecost Arthur was crowned King of Britain.

## *Excalibur*

But then Saxon invaders came from over the sea. The famous Sword in the Stone was broken in a joust. Eleven other chieftains claimed the throne and challenged Arthur.

Arthur was in great danger, so Merlin took him to a secret place high on Bodmin Moor. There was an Enchanted Lake. A hand reached up from the water, holding a sword. It was the Lady of the Lake offering Arthur a magic, unbreakable sword forged by an elf-smith from Avalon. The sword was called Excalibur. With this sword Arthur could not be beaten. He fought twelve great battles, defeated the Saxon invaders and brought peace to the land. You can still visit the lake; it's called the Dozmary Pool.

Tintagel was now well astern. The cliffs seemed endless. The sun grew lower and lower. Tommy recited:

'From Padstow Point to Bideford Bay,
'Tis a watery grave by night and day.'

He sighed, 'There's not enough water to get into Boscastle. We'll have to try for Bude Haven, but it's not safe at night, so we're racing the darkness.'

The sun was already setting when Jamie saw the cliffs end in a broad beach with great rolling breakers.

'That's Widemouth,' said Tommy. 'We can't land there, we'd be scat to pieces.'

It was nearly dark when they sailed into Bude Haven. Behind a tiny breakwater was the smallest of natural harbours. Tommy lowered the mainsail and they ghosted in under foresail alone. They tied to a mooring post and by starlight rowed a dinghy ashore.

*(The moon)*

# 9

NAW

# Bude: Arthur and the Great Boar

*My tail it is curly,*
*My snout it is wet,*
*I eat what you will not,*
*But I am no pet.*

They had landed just in time. Soon they were at the sign of the Falcon, a sailors' boarding house by the river. Anthony told this story.

### Arthur and the Great Boar

One day Arthur and his knights were feasting in their castle at Kelliwik in Cornwall. A bard* was telling tales of Arthur's adventures. Suddenly there was knocking on the door.

It was a Welsh prince called Culhwch, asking for help.

Culhwch had a cruel stepmother. She had put a spell on him so the only lady he could marry was Olwen, the daughter of a bad-tempered and very hairy giant. But the giant would not let her marry unless Culhwch completed a long list of difficult tasks. That's why Culhwch needed Arthur's help.

The hardest task was to get a special comb, razor and scissors to cut the giant's long hair. The trouble was that those things were carried on the head of a hairier and even more bad-tempered giant boar called Twrch Trwyth. It had long tusks and poisonous bristles.

Twrch Trwyth lived in Ireland, but then it swam across the sea to Wales. Arthur and his men chased it right across Wales to the River Severn. Arthur called the knights from Devon and Cornwall to come and help. He said, 'While I live this beast will not enter Cornwall.'

At the River Severn, Arthur's men tripped Twrch Trwyth so it tumbled into the water.

They quickly grabbed the scissors and the razor. But before they could grab the comb the boar leapt up and crossed the river.

Arthur and his men chased it to the west, but it ran so fast they could not catch up till it reached Cornwall. After a mighty struggle they grabbed the comb. Then the knights lined the shore, each with a spear, and marched forward. Twrch Trwyth ran into the sea. It swam off towards Ireland, but no one ever knew where it went.

So Culhwch had the comb, scissors and razor. He was able to cut the giant's hair and marry Olwen. Arthur returned to his castle, back to the feasting hall from which the adventure had begun, and his bard had another story to tell.

Anthony went on, 'They must have caught the boar here in Bude. Further north the cliffs are too steep. The Cornish word for boar is badh.'

Jamie looked at the sea, and imagined Arthur and his knights lining the shore, spears silhouetted against the sky.

*(A pig)*

* bard – a musician, singer and storyteller.

# 10

## PEG

# Davidstow: The Old Goose Woman

*A castle without a door,*
*A soft white bed,*
*Golden treasure within is hid.*

Next day it was too rough to sail, so Anthony decided to walk to Padstow, even though it would take three days. But after just a mile a friendly carter offered them a ride.

'I'm off to Camelford market,' he said.

They swapped stories as the road climbed south. About noon a magnificent vista opened before them; two high hills dominated the horizon.

'What are they?' asked Jamie.

'Router and Bronn Wennili,' said the carter, 'the highest hills in Cornwall*. Mind you, long ago they were higher still.'

## The Old Goose Woman

By the great lakes high in the hills nested the wild geese. There too was the cottage of the old Goose Woman. The geese loved her, for she fed them and kept them safe. In return they would give her goose-eggs, twice as big as hens' eggs.

Their great white wings shaped the clouds and moved the winds, and the Goose Woman smiled at their games. Also, there was another reason she smiled. For it was then that her friend blue-eyed Summer visited, and they would laugh together in the green meadows.

But when the Autumn came, Summer would leave for a warm land far to the south. The Goose Woman would cry many tears.

Then dark-eyed Winter would come. The gentle geese would turn from his cold stares, his icy looks. They would cower from his tempestuous moods. Eventually they would stand no more. Sadly, they would bid farewell to the old Goose Woman and fly to the south. Great ragged skeins* called their sorrow and the cries echoed across the sky.

As the last goose took flight, the Goose Woman would tidy her cottage. With a broom she would sweep the goose feathers through the door to where the wind would take them. She would light her fire and pray for Summer to return.

That was many years ago. Since then the mountains have been worn away by the centuries of tears that have fallen. But the old Goose Woman is still there. As the hills have become lower her cottage is left high in the great Sky-Meadows. You can only visit if you know where the Sky-Stairs are, and that is a great secret.

To this day, when Summer comes, skies are blue, the days are warm, and the geese shape the clouds with their great wings. When he leaves and Winter comes the skies are dark. When the Goose Woman weeps the rain falls. When the geese fly south in ragged skeins across the

*geese fly south in ragged skeins*

sky we know Winter is near, and when the old Goose Woman sweeps the feathers from her cottage, snow falls on the high moors.

Then children remember the bright days. When there is ice on the window, with their fingers they draw little pictures of the Snow Goose, to let the geese know they must come back and bring Summer once again.

*(An egg)*

* these hills are now called Rough Tor and Brown Willy.
* skeins – another word for threads.

# 11

## UNDEG

# Camelford: The Last Battle, Excalibur, The Chough

*I join the choir at matins,*
*My verses reach the sky.*
*I use my quill the heavens to thrill,*
*Tell me, what am I?*

After Davidstow the road descended.

'I enjoyed hearing about King Arthur,' said Jamie. 'What else did he do?'

Anthony thought for a moment.

'After beating the Saxons, he defeated the Danes at Vellandruchar near Sennen. But now we're near Camelford. Some say that's where Arthur fought his last battle.'

## *The Last Battle*

Arthur's wars took him overseas, so he made Mordred, his trusted nephew, Lord of Britain.

But when Arthur was away Mordred imprisoned Arthur's wife, Guinevere. Then when Arthur returned Mordred would not give back the crown.

Arthur pursued Mordred. They fought many battles, but every time, when Arthur was winning, Mordred slipped away in the shadows of defeat. But at Camelford Mordred could not run, for a river and a steep hill prevented retreat. There he made his last stand. After a day of fighting, Mordred impaled Arthur on his lance. But, though badly wounded, Arthur killed the treacherous Mordred with Excalibur. From that day the place was called Slaughterbridge.

## *Excalibur*

Then Arthur called his old friend, Sir Bedivere, and told him to throw Excalibur into the Enchanted Lake from which it had come.

Bedivere took the sword to the water's edge, but it gleamed like ice in moonlight, and he could not bear to throw it away. Instead he hid it in the reeds. When he returned Arthur asked him, 'Did you throw the sword into the lake?'

'Yes,' said Bedivere.

'What happened then?' said Arthur.

'Nothing,' said Bedivere.

'You have not told the truth!' said Arthur. 'A second time I command you, throw the sword into the lake.'

Again Bedivere took Excalibur to the lakeside, but it gleamed like gold in firelight. Again he could not bear to throw it away, so again he hid it. When he returned Arthur asked again, 'Did you throw the sword into the lake?'

'Yes,' said Bedivere.

'What happened then?' said Arthur.

'Nothing,' said Bedivere.

'You have not told the truth!' said Arthur. 'A third time I command you, throw the sword into the lake.'

Then Bedivere took Excalibur to the water's edge. With all his strength he threw the sword high into the air. By now it was sunset. The sword curved through the air; at its highest point it caught the last rays of the sun. The silver cross gleamed against the black sky. As the sword fell towards the lake a lady's arm clad in gleaming white appeared from the water. The hand caught the sword by the hilt, then carried it below without a ripple.

So the Lady of the Lake took back Excalibur. When Arthur asked Bedivere what had happened he told Arthur just what I told you. Arthur knew he was telling the truth.

Then Bedivere heard the sound of singing. As night fell, four fair maidens carried Arthur in a magic boat across the shining sea to Avalon.

## The Chough

In Cornwall you may see a black bird with red legs and beak. Its call is intimate, its flight is hesitant. But it always returns to its roost. That bird is the Chough, the royal bird of Cornwall.

You find its picture on old coats of arms, and that bird is none other than King Arthur.

After his last battle Arthur was not seen again in human form. But he didn't die; he sleeps at Avalon. When he wants to see his old kingdom, he turns into a Chough and flies over his native land. To this day he keeps an eye on Cornwall. If he's ever needed he will return as a warrior to help his countrymen.

So if you see him, greet him in a manner befitting a king. When you see a chough, doff your cap. Say to him, 'Good afternoon, Sire.' After all, he is the once and future king.

As they neared Camelford Jamie saw a small black bird. It had a red beak and red legs. Jamie took off his cap. 'Good afternoon, Sire,' he said.

*(A bird)*

12

DEWDHEK

# St Teath: Anne Jeffries and the Fairies

*Back and forth,*
*In the air.*
*Up and down,*
*Going nowhere.*

Next day they reached St Teath. Anthony went for provisions, leaving Jamie in a garden by the church. Jamie sat on a swing hanging from a tree. Then in the distance he heard a strange ringing sound and musical laughter. He heard leaves rustling and branches moving. In came a girl wearing a smart green dress.

'Hello, I'm Mary,' she said. 'Anthony sent me to tell you a story.'

## Anne Jeffries and the Fairies

Once there was a girl called Anne Jeffries who went to work for a Mr and Mrs Pitt at St Teath.

In those days everyone believed in fairies and Anne longed to meet them. After sunset she looked under fern leaves and into the bells of foxgloves. She sang this song:

> 'Fairy fair and fairy bright,
> Come and be my chosen sprite.'

By moonlight she walked by the stream singing:

> 'Moon shines bright, waters run clear,
> I am here, but where's my fairy dear?'

Anne didn't know, but the fairies were secretly watching.

One day after work she sat on a swing in the garden. She heard branches moving, as if someone was watching her. Then she heard more rustling of branches.

There was a strange ringing sound and musical laughter. Anne heard the gate move. Six little men appeared, smartly dressed in green. They were beautiful, with charming faces and bright eyes. The first had a red feather in his cap. He bowed politely and spoke very kindly.

Anne leaned forward to shake hands. But Feather Cap jumped onto her hand, so she lifted him into her lap. Then he clambered up her front and began kissing her! Anne was charmed as they all climbed up and kissed her. Then a fairy touched Anne's eyes and she could not see. She felt she was flying through the air. Then someone said a magic word and Anne could see again.

She was now in a beautiful place with golden temples and silver palaces, trees with fruits and flowers, and lakes with bright fishes. The air was full of birds with brilliant colours and the sweetest songs. Many ladies and gentlemen walked about; others rested in luxurious bowers with fragrant flowers. Yet more danced or enjoyed games of various kinds.

Anne was now the same size as the little people. She had fine clothes and looked very grand. Her six companions were still with her. Feather Cap was the most attentive but now the others seemed jealous.

Eventually Anne and Feather Cap slipped away on their own and hid in a beautiful bower. But then there was a great commotion. The five other fairies appeared with a great crowd, all very angry. Feather Cap drew his sword to defend Anne but he was soon overcome. Then a fairy touched Anne's eyes and all went dark. She heard strange noises; she felt herself whirled into the air and there was the sound of a thousand flies buzzing round her.

When Anne opened her eyes she was on the ground back in the garden. Many people had gathered round.

They took her indoors and put her to bed. Anne was ill all Autumn, Winter, and Spring. But when she recovered she had magic powers.

Anne's mistress had a sore leg. Anne touched it and it was healed. Then sick people came from miles away. Anne healed them all and took no payment. But she always had pocket money, for the fairies gave it to her.

Anne could tell the future. She always knew who would visit, where they came from, and when they would arrive.

Even stranger, she had no meals from Harvest time to Christmas, but did not starve because she was fed by the fairies.

Anne could become invisible and secretly dance with the fairies in the orchard.

The fairies gave Anne a magic silver cup. Later on she gave it as a present to a little girl called Mary Martyn.

But then the evil magistrate Tregeagle heard of Anne's magic. He threw her into Bodmin jail for communing with evil spirits and told the jailer not to feed her. But Anne was secretly fed by the fairies.

After three months a court found Anne had done nothing wrong. But evil Tregeagle kept her locked up for three months more. But the fairies looked after her until she was set free.

Anne went to live near Padstow. She went on curing people but would never talk about her secrets. Yet to this day there are still some people who have her powers.

Jamie looked doubtful.

*magically filled with clear liquid

'Look,' said Mary. From her apron she took a tiny silver cup that sparkled in the sun. As Jamie watched it magically filled with a clear liquid.

'Anne gave it to me,' she said. Then she slipped back into the bushes. There was the rustling of leaves, musical laughter, and she was gone.

*(A swing)*

# 13

## TARDHEK

# St Breock: Jan Tregeagle

*Golden as hay,*
*Washed twice a day,*
*I slip through your fingers,*
*And keep you at bay.*

Anthony and Jamie followed the River Allen for five miles, then crossed the River Camel at Wadebridge. There soldiers looked at them suspiciously but let them pass.

Beyond the town they reached the hamlet of St Breock. 'That evil Tregeagle lived near here,' said Anthony. 'This is how he met his fate.'

# Jan Tregeagle

As well as a magistrate, Jan Tregeagle was also estate manager for Lord Robartes. But Jan cheated the tenants. He was so evil some said he had sold his soul to the devil. No one was sad when he died.

Then Robartes came to sort things out. He was a kind man; he repaid everyone who had been cheated. Last of all came a farmer. Supposedly he owed some rent. But he put his hand on the Bible and said, 'I swear I paid already. May Tregeagle come and tell the truth!'

There was a clap of thunder and it went pitch dark. As the light returned, there was Jan, as large as life, if a little singed at the edges.

Robartes made him put his hand on the Bible and swear to tell the truth. Then Jan admitted, yes, the farmer had indeed paid the rent.

Then Robartes told Tregeagle to leave. But he said, 'No! I don't want to go back to Hell. Satan is waiting for me.' He couldn't go to

Heaven because of his sins so Jan wanted to stay where he was!

The Abbot of Bodmin was sent for to see what to do. He said that as long as Jan worked for those he had wronged, he could stay on earth. He sent Jan onto Bodmin Moor to empty the Dozmary Pool, as it often overflowed and flooded cottages nearby. But the pool is bottomless and to empty it Jan was given just a limpet shell and, to cap it all, the shell had a hole in it! Some say you can still hear Jan moaning up by the pool.

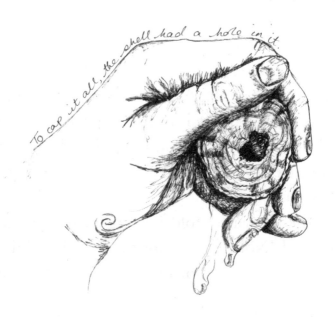

To cap it all, the shell had a hole in it

But the Devil felt cheated. Every night he tried to stop Tregeagle working and so take him back to Hell. He sent rain, thunder and lightning, but nothing could distract Jan from his job.

Finally, the Devil sent his hell-hounds. One leapt up and knocked the shell from Tregeagle's hand into the pool. Jan was now prey for the Devil! He fled across the moor with the hounds close behind. In Lanlivery, near Hellman Tor, they say that sometimes you can still hear them baying.

Next he reached a hermitage* on a rock in the hamlet of Roche. 'Sanctuary!' he cried. The hermit let him in and there the hounds could not touch him, but their snarling was too much for the locals. They too sent for the Abbot of Bodmin.

Jan told the Abbot he'd done his best to empty the pool. So instead of being sent back to Hell he was given a new task: weaving rope from the sands of Padstow's Doom Bar.

Some say he is still there. Every day he weaves a good length, but then the tide comes

in and he starts all over again, quietly weeping the words, 'Ropesss of sssand, ropesss of sssand!'

Ahead was the Padstow estuary. The sea was blue, the sands yellow and bright waves were breaking on the Doom Bar. In the town they met Tommy the fisherman. 'Did you hear?' he said. 'The Carters managed to sink the *Black Prince*, right here in the estuary!'

Soon they were in his cottage, drinking tea and swapping stories.

***(Sand)***

---

\* hermitage: a place where a hermit (a solitary holy man) lives.

# 14

## PESWARDHEK

# Padstow: The Little Horsemen

*Sixty to one are the odds in the race.*
*We never hold hands, but share the same face.*

In Padstow is a building with two little men on horseback on top of the roof. They have stood there for hundreds of years. But at midnight the riders come down and gallop round town. But only one person has ever seen this.

Robin Curgenven was the son of a toymaker. He was nine years old. Once, his parents went to a grown-up's party and left him at home.

Just before midnight Robin woke, climbed out of bed and out of the window and went to

at midnight the riders gallop toward town

the marketplace. There was a full moon and he could see the horsemen clearly. When the clock on St Petroc's Church struck midnight, Robin saw them leap into the street and gallop to the marketplace.

Robin laughed, for they looked just like toys from his father's shop. They galloped round the market and up to the top of the town.

Robin was so excited that he ran after them, forgetting that his feet were bare and that he wore only his nightshirt. He ran fast, but he could not catch them.

Then they turned and on the way back they passed right beside Robin. The second horse was startled to see him and reared up. Its rider dropped his riding crop\*, but then quickly galloped back onto the roof.

Robin went home, but then he found he was not tall enough to climb back in through the window. When his parents returned they found him curled up asleep on the doorstep.

'I saw the horsemen galloping,' said Robin, when his dad carried him inside.

His father thought Robin had been dreaming. But in his hand was clutched a tiny riding crop.

If you look at the horsemen today you will find one holds a riding crop but the other does not.

*(A clock)*

\* riding crop – a short stick used to tap a horse on the flank.

\* the horsemen are now in Padstow museum, but sometimes they escape...

# 15

## PEMTHEK

# Padstow: Davy and the King of the Fishes

*Alone I am only half complete,*
*Knowledge or cunning can me defeat.*

Davy hated fishes.

He hated the taste, the feel and the smell of fish. He hated the expression on their faces when they were on the fishmonger's slab. This was a shame, because the only job he could get was helping the roughest, toughest, most lovable rogue in Padstow, Tommy the fisherman.

Davy hated it, but he had to do it to pay the rent and support his young wife.

Once they sailed out further than ever before: past St Saviour's, past Stepper, past

Pentire, past Newland, past Gulland. They were nearly out of sight of land. There they hove-to. Over the side they put the traditional seven fishing lines. On each line were the traditional seven hooks.

'How many hooks altogether?' asked Anthony. There was a pause. Jamie was saying his times-table in his head.

'Seven sevens are forty-nine.'

Then Tommy and Davy sat down to drink the traditional seven mugs of cocoa. When the cocoa was drunk then they brought in the lines to see what fish they had caught. When Davy got to the last hook on the last line he found a huge fish, its scales were iridescent, they were every colour of the rainbow. He thought, 'I can't kill a beautiful creature like this.'

When he thought Tommy wasn't looking he put it back in the water.

But Tommy turned and saw him.

'I didn't waste my time coming out here for you to throw my profits over the side. You're fired!'

Davy was very sad. He was still sad as he walked up the steep lane to his house. Suddenly there was a flash of light and he found a little man beside him.

'I hear you need a job,' said the little man.

'Why, yes,' said Davy.

'I can help you,' said the man. He clicked his fingers and in his hand appeared some hairy string. He clicked again and on the end of the string appeared a cow.

'This is Betsy,' said the little man. 'She is the best milk cow in Cornwall. Her milk is rich and creamy, her clotted cream is lovely, her milkshakes and ice cream are wonderful. If you had this cow you could open a tea shop. Your problems would be over. Just sign this contract.'

Davy signed the contract. Afterwards he asked, 'What does it say? The print is very small.'

'It says in a year I shall return and ask you three difficult questions. If you get them right you can keep Betsy and you'll never see me again. If you get one wrong then you go to stoke the fires of Hell for eternity.'

There was another flash of light and the man disappeared, leaving Davy holding the string and realising he had just struck a bargain with the Devil.

So Davy took Betsy home. His wife, who was very clever, made their front parlour into a tearoom and soon visitors were pouring in. Betsy was indeed the best milk cow in Cornwall. Her milk was rich, the clotted cream was lovely, the milkshakes and ice cream were wonderful.

But exactly a year later Davy was feeling very worried. He knew the Devil was going to ask him three difficult questions.

There was just one customer in the shop, a man in a shabby coat, drinking tea in the corner.

All day Davy worried about the Devil coming. All day the man in the shabby coat drank tea. Then, just at closing time, there was a flash of light and in came the Devil, with pointed horns, cloven hooves and a long tail.

'Are you ready for your questions?' he asked.

Davy was about to say 'no' when the man in the shabby coat spoke. 'Yes, he is, and that was the first of them.'

'Who asked you?' said the Devil.

'You did,' said the man in the coat. 'And that was your second question.'

By now the Devil was very annoyed. He turned to Davy and said, 'Will you tell that chap to shut up?'

'No, he won't,' said the man in the coat. 'That was your third question, so be on your way!'

The Devil was so annoyed that he somersaulted through the door, stamped his hoof on the pavement, and slid down a crack between the cobbles.

Davy was amazed. 'Thank you,' he said to the man in the coat. 'But why are you here?'

The man stood and took off his coat. Under it he wore a waistcoat. It was iridescent; it was every colour of the rainbow.

'I'm the King of the Fishes,' he said. 'A year ago you saved me, so I came back to save you.'

The two men shook hands and the King of the Fishes walked off towards the harbour.

Davy and his wife danced for joy.

If you want to find their tea shop it's the one with the Devil's hoof-print on the pavement outside. But I think the best way to find it is to find the teashop where the milk is rich, the clotted cream is lovely, and the milkshakes and ice cream are wonderful. Then you will know that's Davy's shop. Out the back, tied up with a piece of hairy string is Betsy, the best milk cow in Cornwall.

*(A question)*

# Bedruthan: The Giant's Steps

*Sisters on a silver road,*
*We never leave our bed.*
*Across and back we always go,*
*But never move our head.*

There was once a giant called Bedruthan. He lived in a cave in the cliffs south of Padstow.

I'm sorry to tell you that Bedruthan was very lazy; also, he hated getting wet. He didn't like washing so he smelled bad and he had potatoes growing behind his ears. When he walked by, the flowers turned away and held their noses.

One day the giants decided to have a feast on Park Head. Invitations were sent to every giant in Cornwall. Bedruthan was pleased because it was not far from where he lived.

The night before the feast he was so excited he couldn't get to sleep. He watched the sun go down and the moon come up. He watched the moon go down and ... then he fell fast asleep.

When Bedruthan woke the sun was high in the sky. He looked at his sundial and saw it was nearly time for the feast. He ran outside and followed the coast northwards. At Carnewas he looked across the bay and saw that his friends were already at Park Head. They were about to start without him.

Bedruthan was desperate. He wanted to take a shortcut across the bay to join his friends, but that would mean getting his feet wet. He shivered with horror at the idea. But he hated missing the start of the party even more.

Then he had an idea, the first for over a hundred years. He reached out and scooped up a great handful of rock and earth and splashed it into the sea. Then he stood on it. Then he scooped up another handful and stood on that; then another and another. That way Bedruthan made stepping stones all the way from Carnewas Point to Park Head so he could join his friends without getting his feet wet.

He arrived just in time. But then his friends said, 'Bedruthan, you smell very bad.' They grabbed his arms and his legs. They counted 'one, two, three,' and tossed him into the sea. Bedruthan splashed and shouted. But when he came out he was clean so he was allowed to join the feast.

Since then the sea has washed away some of his stepping stones, but those left are still called Bedruthan Steps. If you visit, ensure its low tide. Don't swim there, it's not safe.

*(Stepping stones)*

# 17

## SEYTEK

# Crantock and the Dove

*Feet in water,*
*Head in air,*
*The travellers' friend,*
*Going nowhere.*

Next, Anthony and Jamie walked along the coast to Towan Blystra*. They slept in a fish cellar. The following morning they climbed over a rocky headland. Beyond it lay an estuary.

'The River Gannel,' announced Anthony. 'Can you see the bridge?'

Jamie looked, there was no bridge in sight.

'Let's rest,' said Anthony.

Jamie did as he was told.

After a while Anthony said again, 'Now can you see the bridge?'

'No!' said Jamie, feeling annoyed. How could a bridge suddenly appear?

But then he noticed the tide was going out. As the water level fell he saw a line of sticks across the estuary. A little later he could see they made a fence. Then he saw the fence was on one side of a wooden bridge.

Jamie shouted, 'An underwater bridge! That's crazy!'

'But we can cross at low tide,' said Anthony.

After the bridge the path crossed some marsh to a stile below a steep hillside. Jamie saw there was a dove perched on the stile.

'Coo,' it said.

Anthony said, 'This must have been where old Crantock came ashore.'

Jamie knew his dad was about to tell a story.

## Crantock and the Dove

Some call him Carantoc, but we Cornish call him Crantock. He was a holy man from

Wales. He wanted to come here but he didn't have a boat. So he took the altar stone from his chapel, threw it into the sea, jumped in and sailed it to Cornwall. He arrived at this very inlet.

When Crantock came ashore, he was met by a dove that 'coo-ed' in welcome. Crantock saw the steep hillside ahead and said, 'I'm going to settle right here. I don't want to climb that hill.'

Crantock gathered twigs and sticks to make a fire. But he was tired after his long voyage and fell asleep in the sunshine.

When Crantock woke he went to light his fire. But all the twigs had vanished. There was no one in sight, just the friendly dove.

'Bother,' said Crantock, 'I shall just have to have a cold meal.'

'Coo,' said the dove.

Crantock had a miserable, cold supper. Afterwards, for a second time, he gathered twigs for a fire. Then he wrapped himself in a blanket and went to sleep. He woke next morning looking forward to a hot breakfast.

But then he saw the twigs had vanished again. There was still no one in sight, just the same friendly dove.

'Bother,' said Crantock, feeling grumpy.

'Coo,' said the dove.

Crantock looked hard at the dove. For a third time he gathered kindling for his fire. Then, although it was morning, he yawned, wrapped himself in his blanket and closed his eyes.

Five minutes later he suddenly leapt up. There was the dove with a twig in its beak. Crantock tried to grab it but it was too quick. It flew up the hill and Crantock chased it, shouting long words in Welsh.

At the top of the hill Crantock stopped in amazement. There was the dove sitting on a huge pile of twigs. It looked rather smug.

Crantock looked at the dove. The dove looked at Crantock.

'What's going on?' said Crantock.

'Coo,' said the dove.

Crantock looked around. It was a flat, well-drained spot.

'Oh all right,' said Crantock. He built his little chapel on top of the hill and eventually it grew into the church we see today.

Jamie looked up. They had reached the top of the hill. Ahead was a fine upstanding church.

'Coo,' said the dove.

*(A bridge)*

---

* Towan Blystra – the old name for Newquay.

# 18

ETEK

# Perranporth: St Piran

*A field of darkness, four white arms,*
*I sleep in stillness, beckon in storms.*

Soon they reached a magnificent beach.

'There's a saying,' said Anthony, 'there are more saints in Cornwall than in Heaven! Michael was the first saint of Cornwall, for he was seen by Cornish fishermen about 1,500 years ago. Petroc was the next, and this is where Piran came ashore.

'Some say Piran came from Ireland, but it's more likely he was Cornish. Perhaps he went to a seminary in Ireland and then came home. This is the story.'

## *The Coming of St Piran*

Piran worked in Ireland. But one day the High King of Ireland decided that he was deprived. He only had seven wives, poor chap. This was not enough, so he asked another seventeen ladies to marry him. As he was King they all agreed. But when Piran heard about it he told everyone it was wrong.

Next morning the King was in his castle having a magnificent breakfast with his wives and fiancées. When he heard what Piran had said he was very angry. He decided to get rid of Piran.

At that moment Piran was sitting in his hovel eating a frugal breakfast on his own. He knew it was going to be a bad day when soldiers came bursting in.

They dragged Piran to the King, who declared that he should die. Then the King, with his seven wives, seventeen fiancées, household retinue, soldiers, and the entire population marched to the top of the highest cliff in the land. Piran was tied to a millstone and rolled to the cliff edge. 'Do you have any last words?' asked the King.

'I can't swim!' said Piran.

The King replied that the rope and millstone were just in case Piran learned to swim on the way down. Then they rolled the millstone over the edge of the cliff. It landed in the water with the biggest splash imaginable.

But when Piran arrived in the sea, because he was a holy man, the water became holy water. The huge splash soaked everyone on the shore. The King, with his wives, fiancées, household retinue, soldiers and the entire population were all unexpectedly baptized on the spot.

Then the rope tying Piran said, 'This is a holy man, I will not bind him,' so the knots untied themselves.

Then the millstone dragging Piran under water said, 'This is a holy man, I will not drown him,' so the millstone floated to the surface.

Then Piran saw that the King, wives, fiancées, retinue, soldiers and the entire

population were now Christian, having been unexpectedly baptized. Piran's work in Ireland was done and it was time to move on to bigger challenges.

To the east was Cornwall, so Piran waved farewell to the King, the wives, fiancées, and so-on. Having been converted they were now all very fond of Piran, so they wept copiously at his departure. There were so many tears it was like a waterfall and it caused a huge wave. So Piran, stood on his millstone, invented surfing and rode that wave across to Cornwall.

He arrived at a magnificent beach: two miles of perfect sands. Great breakers swept in, gleaming in the sun. It's called Perranporth.

## *St Piran Discovers Tin*

Piran's flag is a white cross on a black background. The black represents the black rock that has the tin inside and the white is the tin itself.

The tale is that when Piran came ashore he was cold, so friendly Cornish people brought firewood and made a fireplace from the local black stones. Soon a fire was blazing. Then Piran noticed a silvery substance flowing from the rocks of the hearth and realised it was tin. Since then Piran has been the patron saint of tinners.

Kernow bys vykken

'It's a good tale,' continued Anthony, 'but they were digging tin in Cornwall 1,500 years before the time of Piran!'

*(Piran's flag)*

# Ladock: The Wrestler and the Demon

*My prayerful mistress wears me in,*
*My master wears me out,*
*A roof upon a roof am I.*
*In wind a roundabout.*

In Ladock lived a wrestler called Jackey Trevail. One Midsummer's day he went to Truro and beat the champion. The prize was a hat laced with gold. But then Jackey boasted, 'I can wrestle anyone, even the Devil himself.'

Jackey went to celebrate with his friends. But on his way home, about midnight, he met someone dressed in black who said, 'I saw the wrestling today. Aren't you the champion?'

'Yes,' replied Jackey, warily.

'I like wrestling,' said the stranger. 'May I wrestle with you, say for your hat and five guineas, which I will stake.'

'Not now,' replied Jackey, 'I'm tired.'

'Then midnight tomorrow,' said the stranger. 'I mustn't be seen; it would not be right.'

Then Jackey thought he saw a cloven foot under the stranger's coat. He remembered what he had said in the ring. He had challenged the Devil and now he suspected that he had met him. But, being polite, Jackey agreed to the challenge. They shook hands and the gentleman gave him a purse with five guineas in it for his stake. He said, 'If by chance I can't come, you can keep the money.'

He said goodbye and left. Poor Jackey was sure he had made a bargain with the Devil, but he could think of no way to avoid his fate.

When Jackey got home his wife Molly came down. She guessed something was the matter. Jackey took out the bag of guineas and threw it into his tool chest, saying, 'Molly, don't touch that bag, it has the Devil's money in it!' Then he told her what had happened.

He finished, 'Oh Molly, you've often wished that Old Nick would take me away and now I think your prayers will be answered.'

'Go to bed,' she ordered. 'I'm going to see Parson Wood.'

The Parson saw Molly coming. 'Please help,' she sobbed. 'Jackey has challenged the Devil and will be carried away if you don't save him!'

Parson Wood replied, 'Tell Jackey to cheer up. I'll tell him what to do.'

Parson Wood went to Jackey's house. He said, 'Jackey, is Molly's tale true, or did you fall asleep on the common and have a bad dream?'

Jackey told him what happened. 'I wish it was just a dream,' he said, 'but the Devil's money is in my tool chest. I remember all he said and I would recognise him again with his fiery eyes and his cloven foot.'

Jackey got the bag. There were the gold pieces.

The Parson studied them and said, 'I'm sure that was the Devil. But take courage, meet him as agreed at midnight.'

Jackey was unhappy; he didn't want to go alone.

'You keep your word,' said the Parson, 'or the Devil may come for you when least expected. I will be close by to protect you.'

Then Parson Wood took from his pocket a slip of parchment on which mystic signs and words from the Bible were written.

'Put this in your waistcoat, over your heart,' he said. 'Wear it when you're wrestling. Don't be frightened, treat him just like any other wrestler, and don't spare him or be fooled by his tricks.'

That night Jackey returned to the common. At midnight the man in black arrived. They looked at each other for some minutes without speaking. Then Jackey said, 'I expect you know the rules. Whoever makes three falls in five bouts wins. You're the challenger, so you start.'

The stranger did not speak but kept staring at him. Jackey said, 'Well, if you won't wrestle, take your money and no harm done.'

That instant Jackey felt himself seized by his waist and lifted off the ground. He felt he was carried high in the air. 'I'm done for!' he cried.

As they struggled Jackey got one arm over his opponent's shoulder. Grabbing him on the back he crooked his leg around the Devil's. But then Jackey's waistcoat touched the Devil, who instantly lost his grip, fell flat on his back, and writhed on the ground like a snake.

Jackey landed on his feet.

The Devil got up, shouting, 'You have a hidden weapon that hurt me; take off that waistcoat!'

'No,' said Jackey, 'I won't! Feel it if you like; there's no blade there, not even a pin. It's you that plays tricks; catch me off-guard if you can.'

Then he grabbed the Devil and they wrestled for five minutes, pushing and pulling. But although the Devil seemed afraid to close in, Jackey was frightened by the Devil's evil eyes and couldn't get a crook with his legs. So he backed off and then surprised the

Devil with a 'flying-mare', throwing him on his back with a thump.

The Devil sprang up, very angry, saying, 'You have fooled me and you are very rough. Tell Parson Wood to go home. I am confused and powerless whilst he is watching.'

'I don't see the Parson, just you,' said Jackey.

'I can see his eyes glaring between the bushes,' replied the Devil, 'and I hear him mumbling. If I lose, it will be your Parson's fault. I shall punish him for this.'

'Never mind our Parson, he can wrestle very well himself,' said Jackey, now feeling cheerful. 'He likes to see a good match; so let's start again.' With this, Jackey grasped the Devil in a 'Cornish hug' and laid him on his back as flat as a flounder. Then Jackey said, 'You have had three falls; but if that's not enough, I can show you more.'

Jackey watched the Devil, ready to give him another thump. For a while he crawled on the ground like a snake. Then clouds hid the moon. The Devil's feet and legs become like those of a huge bird, his cloak became

wings, and he turned into a dragon. Then he flew away, skimming the ground and leaving a trail of fire. He soared up into the clouds. They became ablaze with lightning and thunder echoed from hill to hill. The cloud ascended, whirling like a tornado, flashing lightning and shooting thunderbolts.

Then Jackey heard the Parson say, 'Well done. Take your prizes and let's go home.'

Parson Wood gave Jackey breakfast. Jackey said, 'I shall be glad to serve you at any hour, day or night, for I owe you more than life.'

'Not so,' the Parson replied. 'I have only done my duty, guarding from the wolf a slightly thoughtless member of my flock.'

Jackey still has the hat laced with gold.

*(A hat)*

# 20

UGENS

# The Feathered
# Fiend of Ladock

*Seldom stand, never walk,*
*Scream and shout, never talk.*

A good peal of bells will warn off any devil. But the Ladock bells were silent because their ropes were worn and the bell frame was rickety.

Soon after Jackey's victory an evil spirit in the form of a huge bird came and perched on Ladock Church tower. It had coal-black feathers and fiery eyes, and it made a terrible din, especially during church services.

When Parson Wood entered it laughed out loud. During quiet prayers it would screech like a pig caught in a gate. People burst out laughing; some laughed so much they had to leave.

When the choir sang psalms, the Feathered Fiend made wailing noises. Once it distracted the Clerk so that instead of the psalm he sang a ballad instead. No one knew if they should sing 'Glory Be' at the end or not.

At the confession the Fiend copied the cackling of old women. When the Parson spoke it made very rude noises. When everyone stood to leave, it gave the cry of hounds in full chase.

The Parson was sure the Fiend had been sent by the Devil in revenge for helping Jackey. It was out of reach of his whip and exorcism failed. Everyone was fed up. Then one Sunday, after church, the Parson said to the Clerk, 'During today's sermon, when the Fiend made a noise like a cow stuck in the mud, I had an idea.'

'Yes?' asked the Clerk.

'You know what it says in the Bible about little children,' continued Parson Wood, 'also old folks have a saying: the Evil One can't stand the sight of an innocent child.

'Newly baptised children have the greatest power to drive away evil spirits. Tomorrow you must ask all women who have recently had babies to come to church next Sunday afternoon and have them christened.'

So the next day the Clerk went round the parish. He found eight mothers with un-baptized children.

'Well done,' said Parson Wood. 'As twelve is a very lucky number, we will make a dozen by adding four babies christened last year.'

So next Sunday twelve mothers came with their babies and the godparents. The Feathered Fiend was still on the tower, being very rude.

The eight new babies were christened. Then the Parson walked out of church, followed by all twelve mothers with their babies and the godfathers and godmothers, in a procession. Then they lined up opposite the belfry.

Then Parson Wood told each mother to pass her child from one godparent to another, the last handing it to him. He then held the child up so that the Devil could see it, then he gave it back. Then the mothers held up their babies whilst the Parson walked to and

fro, reading scriptures and making mystical signs in the air with his staff. He went on for a long time, in a loud voice. But the Feathered Fiend took no notice; it seemed that the Parson had failed.

But then one of the babies started crying. Then all the others cried too. Each one tried to cry the loudest. The Parson spoke ever louder. The Feathered Fiend looked down.

It gave a deafening scream and flew straight up in the air. With every flap of its huge wings there were sparks and blue flames. Then, flying west, it disappeared.

The Feathered Fiend never returned and there was great rejoicing. The bells were mended and their peals now keep all fiends well away. We should never complain about the noise of church bells, nor the crying of a baby.

*(A baby)*

# 21

## ONAN WARN UGENS

# The Battle
# of Penryn

*Wings have I but never fly,*
*My clothes are always lent,*
*People seldom pass me by,*
*My words are never meant.*

Next morning Jamie led his dad into the town of Truro. There a friendly boatman offered them a ride. They sailed down the Truro River into the Fal. Three hours later they were ashore in Penryn, climbing the main street to the King's Arms.

'Welcome,' said the landlord, 'to the oldest inn in Cornwall.'

'How old?' asked Jamie, innocently.

The landlord frowned, '500 years!'

Jamie looked unconvinced.

'We are very historical!' he said. 'I'll tell you about the Battle of Penryn.'

'I was a soldier,' exclaimed Anthony, 'but I never heard of the Battle of Penryn.'

'Listen!' said the landlord. 'It was like this.'

## *The Battle of Penryn*

In 1595 the Spanish sent ships and soldiers who burned Mousehole, Paul, Newlyn and Penzance. They boasted about it to the King of Spain.

But they *didn't* say they had been too scared to land at St Eval and Padstow. There the men were at sea, but the women put on red flannel petticoats above their underskirts. They marched to the cliff tops where the raiders thought they were Redcoats* and sailed away. Neither did they mention the Battle of Penryn, and I'm not surprised!

Now the people of Penryn have always been cultural! That's why the old Cornish-language plays flourished here. So when a travelling theatre visited Penryn in 1595 everyone was there, enjoying the play. Even the King's Arms closed for the performance.

A stage was erected right across the street at the marketplace, so people could watch from the street above. The play was *Edward IV* by Thomas Heywood. There was a murmur in the audience as a spectacular scene depicting the Battle of Tewkesbury grew near.

But that very night the Spanish navy anchored in the Penryn River. There they found the first Cornish defence.

'What was that?' asked Jamie.

'Mud,' said the landlord. 'The tide was out. They had to anchor in deep water, so their cannon were out of range of the town. Then they had to wade ashore through acres of the stickiest mud in the land.'

Then, soaked to the skin, muddy, smelly and rather worried, the Spaniards crept into Penryn.

To their surprise the place seemed empty. There were no lights, no sounds, no movement. Immediately they suspected a trap.

Warily the Spaniards climbed Broad Street, past the King's Arms. Looking up to the market place, in the starlight they saw what looked like a barricade across the road. Beyond it they could faintly hear voices. Flickering lights were seen. They suspected that the Cornish had seen them coming and organised their defence.

Then, on the uphill side of the stage, the citizens of Penryn cheered as warlike music announced the Battle of Tewksbury. They cheered louder when trumpeters sounded the advance. On stage the order 'Fire the cannon!' was given. Two ancient guns, laden with gunpowder and wadding, were detonated. There were huge bangs, and the audience bayed its approval. Actors fired imitation muskets and charged across the stage. The audience cheered again.

The Spanish marines, every nerve taut, heard the martial music, then the cheering of hundreds of voices. They thought a Cornish army was waiting for them.

Next the Spaniards heard an artillery captain ordering his guns to fire. They ducked as two huge explosions rent the air. Then they heard the sound of muskets, swords drawn from scabbards, the shouts and cheers of many hundred men. Beyond the barricade they saw the flash of gunfire.

On the road near the King's Arms there was no cover. The houses either side seemed ideal for a Cornish ambush. The only safe route was back down to the river. The cheering and gunfire grew louder. The cannons sounded again.

The Spaniards retreated, sure it was a trap. They were so noisy that the audience heard them and chased them down the hill.

Then the Cornishmen stopped and laughed as the Spaniards waded through mud up to their waists and clambered back into their boats. As they sailed away the locals returned to the King's Arms to celebrate the Battle of Penryn.

It was the best evening's entertainment Penryn had ever known. No one was hurt and a brave time was had by all.

*(A theatre)*

\* redcoats – British soldiers.

# 22

# DEW WARN UGENS

# The Ghost of Stithians

*I cover my lady,*
*I cover my lord.*
*No crime have I done,*
*But I'm taken and hung.*

Above Penryn they walked towards Stithians.
At dusk they reached the woods of Kennall Vale.

'We could shelter under a tree,' said Jamie.

'That would be cold,' said Anthony.

Then they heard scrabbling in the bushes,
followed by a giggle.

'I know you're there,' Jamie shouted. 'Come
out!'

There were more giggles. Then from the
bushes came two children. There was a girl,

older than Jamie, and a boy who was a bit younger. Both were smiling.

'We tracked you for miles,' said the boy.

'Yards,' said the girl. 'I'm Ellie; this is Charlie. Who are you?'

Anthony smiled. 'I am Anthony James. This is my son Jamie. I'm a storyteller.'

'Grampa told us about you,' said Charlie. 'He tells stories too.'

'I should like to meet him,' said Anthony.

'It's nearly dark,' said Ellie.

'We're all right,' Jamie replied.

Ellie frowned. 'No you're not. I can tell, you have nowhere to go.'

'You can stay in our den!' said Charlie.

The children led them into the wood. The den was under a large tree. The roof was made of branches. On the floor were dry ferns and outside was a fireplace.

Charlie and Ellie brought potatoes. They all sat by the fire whilst they roasted.

'Where are you going next?' asked Ellie.

'Stithians,' said Anthony. 'Where the ghost came from,' and he began a story.

## *The Ghost of Stithians*

Near Stithians lived a widow called Jenny Hendy. She had a cousin called Rob. He did jobs for her and she kept his savings safe in her wooden chest. She said she would add to them when he got married. In her will she left everything to Rob. But then old Jenny died.

After the funeral Rob opened the chest but it was empty. No one knew where Rob's savings or Jenny's money had gone. The only way to find out was to get Tammy, the white witch of Helston, to ask Jenny's ghost.

Tammy agreed to help for two sovereigns, one in advance. When Rob rode to Stithians he felt scared and wanted to go home, but then he met Tammy. She mumbled strange words. When asked she said, 'Quiet! I'm asking the spirits to call Jenny. You're not scared, are you?'

'No,' lied Rob.

Near the church Tammy said, 'Here's a dangerous spirit I must subdue or it may haunt us. You're not scared, are you?'

'No,' lied Rob.

At the lych-gate he heard unearthly howls, yells and the hooves of a horse. Tammy said, 'Old Nick and his headless hounds are often here. You're not scared, are you?'

'No,' lied Rob.

'We must take care!' said Tammy, 'When Jenny's spirit is raised, no one may be able to lay it again! She may carry you off. Such things often happen!'

Rob was terrified.

'Let's go home,' he said, 'you keep the money.'

'Speak to the ghost!' she said. 'But you must give me the other sovereign, so I can lay her to rest. Otherwise she will haunt you for ever.'

The noises were louder still. Rob shook with fright. 'Let's go,' he said, giving the witch another coin.

Then Tammy gave a great cry. 'I'm telling the spirits that I shan't want them any more tonight,' she said.

Rob and the witch rode home. Tammy said, 'Jenny's ghost may come here. If that happens send for me; I'll do my best to calm her.'

From then on Rob was always scared. He often heard Jenny's ghost rattling pans in the dairy. One day, outside, he saw a ghost waving to him. He was about to run when the ghost said, 'Hello, Rob. Don't you recognise me? I just left my ship in Falmouth. How are you?'

'Jack!' said Rob. 'I was so mazed* I thought you were a ghost.' It was Robin's cousin, who was a sailor.

Jack said, 'I heard that Jenny died and her ghost can't rest. What happened?'

Rob described the spirits in the churchyard, the devil, the clatter of hooves, the howling of hounds.

But Jack said, 'I think those ghosts were conjured up by your fears and fancies. I bet Tammy was trying to frighten you. Let's visit her. I'm a distant cousin of Jenny; I too can ask what happened to her money!' So off they went.

At Tammy's house, Jack said he would pay well and she agreed to help. He gave her a sovereign in advance.

Next evening Jack met Tammy. Again she mumbled strange words. She said, 'I am asking the spirits to call Jenny. You're not scared, are you?'

'No,' said Jack.

Near the churchyard Tammy said, 'Here's a dangerous spirit I must subdue, or it may haunt us. You're not scared, are you?'

'No,' said Jack.

At the lych-gate he heard unearthly howls, yells and the hooves of a horse. Tammy said, 'Old Nick and his headless hounds are often here. You're not scared, are you?'

'No,' said Jack.

'We must take care!' said Tammy. 'When Jane's spirit is raised, no one may be able to lay it again! She may carry you off. Such things often happen!'

Jack guessed Tammy was trying to frighten him.

Then, with her staff, the witch drew a circle on the ground around Jack. She said, 'This magic ring will protect you. Whatever happens, don't leave it.'

Then she pointed her staff towards Jenny's tomb. She commanded, 'Spirit of Jenny

Hendy, by the spirits of fire, air, earth, and water, rise from the grave!' She ended with a shriek.

She did this three times. From the grave there were fearful sounds, like the breaking of wood and stones, and moans, groans, and shrieks. 'Behold!' said Tammy, pointing to the grave.

A ghostly figure in a white shroud rose and came towards Jack. He saw its ashen face, its grisly locks, its glaring eyes. Jack stepped outside the circle of protection!

The ghost called, 'Why do you disturb my rest? I will haunt you for the rest of your miserable life.' But then it ended with, 'The devil take me if I don't!' in a distinct Cornish accent. Then it reached out and seized Jack.

But Jack had heard the very human end of its speech. Also, the ghost's breath smelt of gin, and it hiccupped in a very human way. Jack punched it on the nose and it fell to the ground.

But then Tammy hit Jack with her staff. He wrenched the stick from her. He saw the

ghost stand again, but its shroud had come off. It was Jemmy, Tammy's husband.

'You villain!' said Jack. 'I will thrash you for frightening Rob and swindling him. You must return our sovereigns.'

'Mercy,' cried Jemmy.

Tammy said, 'Don't kill the poor ghost!' and gave back the money.

Jack said, 'You are two rogues.'

'We are sorry,' said Tammy, 'but we couldn't help it. Everyone knows Rob asked me to raise Jenny. Let's say that her ghost came, she knows who has the money, and unless it's returned she will come and haunt them.'

Jack agreed and headed home. On the way he met Rob.

'I've seen the ghost!' said Jack. Then he explained that it was really Jemmy and he described the plan.

In the inn they told everyone that Jenny's ghost had been raised and she knew who took the money. They said the ghost would haunt the thieves forever unless the money was returned. Gossips carried the story everywhere. Those who had taken Jenny's money were so frightened that they all gave it back.

But once Jack returned to sea, Rob heard noises every night. This was not a pretend ghost, it was real. It was as if Jenny wanted him out, so he often visited the town. There he met a charming young lady and soon they were married. That very day a gale stripped some loose thatch from the roof. In the hole was a satchel, with Jenny's savings and lots more. Then the real ghost left and they lived happy ever after.

*(A cloak or a sheet)*

* mazed – a word meaning befuddled and cofused.

# 23

# TREI WARN UGENS

# Praze: Sam Jago's Last Day at School

*I point to heaven, I point to hell,*
*But I am neither spire nor well.*

After a comfortable night in the den Jamie led the way towards Praze. There a kindly miner's wife gave them tea and saffron buns. This was her story.

### Sam Jago's Last Day at School

Old Sam Jago was a good tin miner. But he had never been to school and was no good at sums. When asked what was two plus two he would answer 'not enough thumbs'. When asked six plus six he would reply 'not enough fingers'. If his wife, Jenefer, sent him to the baker's shop for saffron buns he never got the money right.

So when Sam retired, Jenefer said, 'You are useless at sums. I'm sending you to school.'

Next day Sam went to school. It was not very comfortable because the stools were small, and his legs stuck out under the desk. The children laughed at his long beard and his grey hair.

When the teacher asked him what was two plus two he said 'not enough thumbs'. All the children laughed and shouted 'four!'

When the teacher asked him what was six plus six he replied 'not enough fingers'. The children laughed again and cried 'twelve!'

By tea time Sam was very fed up.

Next day it was the same, and the day after too. By the end of the third day Sam had a sore bottom from perching on a tiny stool, and his legs ached from sticking out straight. He walked home grumbling, 'I'm not going back there.'

Then round the corner galloped a horse ridden by a rich young man. Sam jumped into the ditch to avoid being ridden down. The horse reared up on its hind legs and a leather satchel fell from the saddle. But the rider just galloped on.

Sam rescued the satchel and called out, but the rider did not hear him. So Sam took it home.

'I'm not going back to school,' he said to Jenefer. 'The kids just laugh at me, and I've got a sore bottom and stiff legs. This is the day that I leave school.'

Jenefer was about to scold him when she saw the satchel.

'What's that?' she asked.

Sam explained about the young man on the horse and Jenefer said, 'He's bound to come back. We'll keep it safe on top of the wardrobe in our bedroom until he comes calling.'

Two weeks later there was a knock at the door. There was the young man. He spoke to Sam.

'Now then, you old fool, have you ever found anything lying in the lane?'

'Yes, sir,' said Sam, rather upset at the young man's rudeness.

'When was that?' asked the young man.

Sam fumbled with his fingers, trying to count how many days ago it had been.

'Quick!' said the young man impatiently.

'Not enough fingers,' said Sam.

'Surely you know?'

Sam suddenly smiled, ''Twas the day I left school.'

The young man studied Sam's grey hair and long beard.

'The day you left school?' said the young man. 'That must have been fifty years ago! Whatever you found you can keep. I wasn't born then.'

The young man stormed out of the door and rode away.

Sam and Jenefer got the satchel from the top of the wardrobe. Inside was a hundred pounds.

'Keep it, that's what he said,' smiled Sam.

The young man never returned to claim his money, and Sam never returned to school.

*(Tin mine)*

# 24

## PAJAR WARN UGENS

# St Ives: John Knill

Soon they passed a reedy estuary and an hour later they reached the fishing town of St Ives. On the headland Jamie saw a man with a telescope, looking out to sea. He smiled and waved. It was John Knill, the Exciseman, watching for privateers and smugglers. It was he that had spotted the *Black Prince* and sent the Carters after it.

Anthony chanted:

As I was going to St Ives,
I met a man with seven wives,
Each wife had seven sacks,
Each sack had seven cats,
Each cat had seven kits:
Kits, cats, sacks, and wives,
How many were there going to St Ives?

'Has Mr Knill really got seven wives?' asked Jamie.

'No,' laughed Anthony, 'it's just a riddle.'

Jamie said, 'Seven wives and seven sacks? Seven sevens is forty-nine. Seven cats and seven kits; that's forty-nine too. But I can't multiply forty-nine and forty-nine, it's too hard. What's the answer?'

watching....

'One,' said Anthony.

'One?' shouted Jamie, 'Why?'

'Listen again,' said Anthony. 'Listen to what the rhyme actually says.'

So he did.

# 25

# PEMP WARN UGENS

# Zennor: Betsy and the Bell

*Hung with my brothers,*
*We sing together.*
*Pull my tail, I'll do it again.*

Above St Ives the view was magnificent. The bay was a bright turquoise colour; farther out the sea was dark blue; the breakers were intensely bright. The track wound between moor and cliff and soon they reached Zennor.

But there, there was shouting and arguing. A team of bell ringers had come to ring the bells of Saint Senara.

'The finest peal in Cornwall,' said the local Bell Captain.

'How can that be if one of your bell ropes isn't long enough?' argued one of the visitors.

'It's not that the rope isn't long enough,' said the Bell Captain. 'It's that your arms are too short!'

Eventually a very tall ringer was assigned to the short rope and the bells were rung. It was indeed a fine peal, even if one of the bells was, as they say, 'three scats behind.' Afterwards the Bell Captain told this story.

### Betsy and the Bell

'Twas long ago. The folk of Zennor heard that a great storm was coming. They shuttered the windows, closed the doors and drove the animals up onto high ground. All apart from Betsy the milker. She broke the hairy string that tethered her behind the henwife's cottage and she wouldn't be caught for love nor money. Eventually they gave up trying and went home.

The storm arrived, just as they thought. It lasted for three days. But then, when it was over, the villagers were summoned from their houses by the sound of a church bell. But they knew everyone was indoors. Who was ringing the bell? Nobody knew; perhaps it was the Devil. But you can't be too careful with such things, so the villagers lined up behind the priest. He took a crucifix in one hand and a Bible in the other and led them to the church. The door was swinging eerily on its hinges.

They stopped and said a prayer. Nervously they stepped into the church. It was dark and silent. Then they sensed movement from the tower and gazed into the shadows. Two horns came into sight. An old lady screamed, 'It's the Devil himself!' and fainted. The priest reached for his flask of holy water.

Suddenly there was a loud 'moo' and from the shadows trotted Betsy, who was delighted to have some human company.

When the storm had arrived, Betsy found the only open door in the village was the church door, left ajar by the absent-minded churchwarden. Betsy went inside, but then she felt hungry. The only edible thing in the church was the tail of the bell rope. So she started nibbling it. She nibbled happily for three days, but then the rope-end was above her head height, so whenever she chewed she rang the bell.

It's been left like that ever since – a memorial to the great storm and the cow that rang the bell.

'And,' ended the Bell Captain, 'what's good enough for Betsy is good enough for anyone!'

*(A bell)*

# 26

# HWEGH WARN UGENS

# Zennor: The Mermaid of Zennor

*I see you,*
*You see you,*
*You see me,*
*But I do not.*

'But how,' asked Jamie, 'did the people of Zennor know the storm was coming?'

'Well,' said the Bell Captain, 'it's like this.'

### The Mermaid of Zennor

Under the sea, between the Lizard and the Isles of Scilly is the lost land of Lyonesse, drowned by a great storm long ago. There were woods, fields and 140 parish churches.

It stretched far to the west with a watchtower at the farthest point.

Old folks say that when such a storm is about to happen again, you can hear the bell of the drowned village of Chy an Mor ringing out a warning and *no good will come of it*.

In Zennor there lived Mathy Trewhella. Every Sunday he rang the bell in church and sang in the choir. He sang so well people came miles to hear him. More people listened to him than to the rector. The old folk of Zennor said that his singing could entrance a mermaid, *but no good will come of it*.

One day a young lady joined the congregation. She had green eyes and long golden hair. She sat on her own at the back of the church and spoke to no one. But she listened intently whenever Mathy sang. Soon rumours spread that Mathy had been seen walking out with this young lady, and everyone was pleased for them. All but the old folks. They said, '*No good will come of it*!'

Then one day Mathy vanished. Never again did he ring the bell in church or sing in the choir. He and the golden-haired girl were never seen again. The old people cried, 'We said *no good would come of it!*'

Later people heard a bell ringing beneath the sea. The tolling of the bell seemed familiar. Some said it was the bell of Chy an Mor warning of a great storm. They pulled the boats up the beach, shuttered the windows and barred the doors. Then the greatest storm they had ever known arrived. The old people grumbled, '*No good will come of it!*' but everyone was safe.

As the storm died a sea captain rode into town. 'News!' he said. 'I anchored my ship off St Ives to shelter from the storm. As it abated I heard someone calling. I looked over the rail and there was a mermaid with golden hair and green eyes. "Move your ship," she said. "The anchor is lying across the entrance to my home, and soon my husband Mathy will return from tolling the bell of Chy an Mor. He will want to come in for his supper."'

'Is that Mathy Trewhella?' asked the captain.

*the anchor was across the entrance of their home*

'Yes,' said the mermaid. 'He lives with me under the sea and whenever a storm is coming he will toll a warning to his friends in Zennor on the great bell of Chy an Mor.'

So Zennor learned the fate of Mathy Trewhella. A picture of the mermaid was carved on a pew in Zennor Church. It's still there, and the old people still say, '*No good will come of it*!'

*(A mirror)*

# 27

# SEYTH WARN UGENS

# St Just: The Wrestlers of Carn Kenidjack

*One at the top,*
*Two at the bottom.*
*My master often,*
*My mistress seldom.*

In St Just Jamie guided his dad to the Star Inn. From inside came a merry tootling sound.

'It's Frosty,' said Anthony.

'But it's July!' laughed Jamie.

'It's Frosty Foss playing his oboe. His real name is Billy, but only his mother calls him that.' Anthony and Jamie took out their fiddles and joined in. Then the landlady brought Frosty a drink and he stopped playing.

'Even I can't blow and suck at the same time,' he said. Then he turned to Anthony: 'Last year you gave me a story, and my rule is this, within a year and a day I have to give it back, to show I can pass it on properly.' Anthony smiled broadly and the room fell silent as Frosty began.

## The Wrestlers of Carn Kenidjack

Jacky and Jan were two poor mining lads. They were so poor they didn't even have a belt between them to hold up their trousers. Those trousers were held up with hairy string left over from tying up the corn at harvest time. On Fridays they looked forward to meeting their friends in the Kiddlywink*. But the lads lived in St Just and then, unlike today, there was not one alehouse in the town. To wet your whistle you had to walk four miles to Morvah.

One Friday evening Jacky and Jan were about to set out when their mother, old Ma

Curgenven, called them. 'Do you know what night it is?' she asked. They shook their heads. They had no idea what night it was. She said, 'Tonight is hallowe'en, when you may see *ghosts, ghouls, goblins, and even old Nick himself.* You must be home by midnight.'

The lads promised and set off to Morvah. Down the hill and across the stream at Nancherrow, then up past Botallack and Pendeen, quickly skirting Carn Kenidjack, for there you can see flickering lights and hear wild hooting sounds – the work of *ghosts, ghouls, goblins, and even old Nick himself.*

Soon they reached the Kiddly and were swapping songs and stories. Because it was hallowe'en they were all about *ghosts, ghouls, goblins, and even old Nick himself.*

It was so much fun they did not notice the time passing. Suddenly the clock said midnight and the lads knew they were in awful trouble. They put down their glasses and ran down the road. They thought, 'If we're only a bit late then we'll only be in a bit of trouble.' Then they thought, 'If we took a shortcut across the Gump, just below Carn Kenidjack, we would be in even less trouble.' So they left the road on the shortcut. But only minutes later they heard the sound of a horse galloping towards them. It was so fast they had to throw themselves off the path to avoid being ridden down.

Jacky shouted, 'That's no way to ride at night!'

The horse stopped. The rider wore a cloak with tall collar, but they could see his eyes glowing red in the dark. He said, 'I'm going up Carn Kenidjack to watch the wrestling. Why don't you come too?'

Now there's no sport a Cornish lad likes more than wrestling. Suddenly it seemed the most natural thing in the world to follow the commanding stranger up the hill (though I don't want to hear of you doing anything as foolish as that!).

At the top of the carn the lads found a grassy bank surrounding a plen an gwary, a playing place. In the middle of this ring were two huge wrestlers, and watching them were *ghosts, ghouls, goblins, and even old Nick himself,* with his eyes still blazing red.

Then the wrestling began. It was like no match you've ever seen. The wrestlers were ten feet tall. With every fall you could hear the cracking of bones, the ripping of sinews, and the tearing of flesh. It was like St Just on Friday night.

Eventually one of the wrestlers lifted the other into the air and smashed him down onto the ground. The watchers lifted the winner onto their shoulders and carried him to old Nick.

But the loser just lay motionless on the ground. 'We must help him,' said Jacky. The lads scrambled into the arena.

'Is he alive?' asked Jacky.

'Just,' said Jan.

'We must get a doctor,' said Jacky.

'I think it's too late,' replied Jan.

'What about a priest?' asked Jacky.

'There isn't time,' said Jan.

'Do you know any prayers?' asked Jacky.

'I know one,' said Jan, and he started. 'Our Father, who art in heaven ...'

Then he stopped. On the back of his neck all the little hairs were standing on end, the feeling you get when you know you're being watched. The lads turned round and RIGHT BEHIND THEM were all the *ghosts, ghouls, goblins, and even old Nick himself*, and he was not happy.

Old Nick raised his arm, he pointed his crooked finger straight at them, his chest heaved as he drew breath, he opened his mouth to speak. But the lads didn't wait to hear what he said. They ran as fast as they could down towards St Just. Behind them came all the *ghosts, ghouls, goblins, and even old Nick himself*. But with every yard the ghosts got closer.

Jacky and Jan knew that ghosts dare not cross running water. If they could get over the bridge at Nancherrow they would be safe.

But then Jacky had the stitch and the ghosts were getting very close.

Then Jan's laces came undone and the ghouls were closer still.

I wish this tale had a happy ending. But they were one pace from the bridge when the biggest, hungriest goblin reached out his hairy hands and seized them BOTH by the seat of the pants. He opened his jaws to BITE their heads off.

But Jacky and Jan were just poor mining lads. Their trousers were held up with hairy string.

There was a mighty twang; the string broke. Jacky and Jan crossed the bridge but their trousers never did.

At home old Ma Curgenven was waiting on the doorstep. When she asked why they had come home at one in the morning with no trousers on, this story was what they told her.

*(Trousers)*

---

\* kiddlywink – a beer or cider house, also called a kiddly for short.

# Mousehole: Tom Bawcock

*A tree tossed in a ploughed field,*
*The wind tugs at my shirt.*
*Salt slips through my many claws,*
*And tumbles round my skirt.*

Soon they reached the port of Mousehole\*. In the Ship Inn they shared a fish pie. After the meal Anthony said to Jamie, 'It's your turn!'

So Jamie began, 'Once upon a time…'

### Tom Bawcock

The winter storms were the worst Cornwall had ever known. The narrow entrance to the harbour of Mousehole was impassable.

Breakers swept across it, and out at sea the waves were big enough to sink any ship. No one had been able to go fishing. It was nearly Christmas, but everyone was starving.

Now a fisherman called Tom Bawcock lived in Mousehole. He was a good seaman. Two days before Christmas, Tom decided he would take a chance. He said it was better to risk drowning while trying to catch something, than starve to death doing nothing.

Tom summoned up his courage. Saying a prayer to St Michael, he sailed boldly out of the harbour just after a wave passed. Then he bore away to gain steerage way before the next wave arrived.

He had only set a tiny sail, but the wind was so strong that he struggled to keep his boat upright and under control. But somehow he made his way to windward, dodging the breakers. Over the side he trailed seven lines, each with seven hooks.

When he had sailed as far as he dared he hove to and pulled in the lines. On each line was a different sort of fish. There were Morgi (dog fish), Lances (sand eels), Fair Maids (pilchards), Ling (a sort of cod), Hake, Scad, and Mackerel.

Tom tacked round. He sailed up to windward, for down to leeward were the St Clement's Rocks. Then Tom bore away to get up speed. As he came rushing in the biggest wave you can imagine picked him up and carried him towards the rocks. But Tom judged it perfectly, surged past the rocks and came flying into the harbour entrance.

In Mousehole everyone cheered old Tom.

Fisher-lasses took the seven sorts of fish and made a huge pie. To decorate it the fish heads were left sticking up, so it was called a Starry-Gazey Pie.

Ever since, Mousehole celebrates the 23rd of December as Tom Bawcock's eve and they eat Starry-Gazey Pie.

*(Fishing boat)*

* Mousehole is actually pronounced 'Mowzel'.

# 29

# NAW WARN UGENS

# Marazion: St Michael and the Mount. Cormoran's Breakfast

*What secrets lie between my leaves,*
*Alone I cannot tell.*
*But at my parting you may find,*
*What once was hidden well.*

Next day they set off early, skirting inland round Newlyn and Penzance.

'I'm not going there again,' said Anthony. Jamie remembered how the hard-hearted magistrate, Henry Boase, had once locked them up just because he didn't like travellers.

It didn't take long to reach Marazion, close to St Michael's Mount and Anthony told this tale.

## St Michael and the Mount

Many years ago the angels' chief warrior, Archangel Michael, fought with the Devil and stopped him from dropping hell-fire on the people of Helston. After the battle Michael was tired and wanted a rest. On the top of a rocky mount off the Cornish coast, he found a natural chair in the rock. It was just the right size and was very comfortable.

This chair became St Michael's favourite place. He often sat there, watching boats from Newlyn and Mousehole. He grew fond of the Cornish fisherman as he heard them singing and telling tall tales whilst sailing to the fishing grounds.

One day as Michael sat in his chair the fog came down. In the gloom he heard the voices of Cornish fishermen struggling to find their way home.

Michael remembered all the dangerous rocks nearby: Hogus, Ryeman, the Cressars, and the Mount itself. He stood up and shouted a warning. The fisherman were startled to hear Michael's great voice. They looked up and saw him pointing towards clear water. His great wings flapped and the fog cleared. Thanks to Michael they sailed safely home.

his wings flapped and the fog cleared.

Since that day Cornish fishermen have known that Michael is watching over them. That is why Michael is the saint of Cornish fishermen and one of Cornwall's patron saints, alongside Petroc and Piran.

There was applause. Jamie looked behind him. A group of ragged children had gathered to listen, so Jamie told them the following story.

### Cormoran's Breakfast

Cormoran the giant was grumpy. In fact, he was downright bad tempered. This was quite normal. Giants are not known for their sense of humour, and Cormoran, of all the giants in Cornwall, was quite the grumpiest. He was also the biggest, smelliest, and hungriest. Every morning when he woke he was hungry, and so every morning he was especially bad tempered.

'Hrrmph!' thought Cormoran one day. 'I need breakfast.'

He got out of his bed, knocking aside various fleas, rats, ferrets and dogs that also slept there. He didn't wash, he didn't brush his tooth (he just had one very big tooth); he just put on his dirty clothes and set off.

This is the point I can tell you that, although he was very grubby, rather surprisingly, Cormoran had clean feet. They were gleaming. This was because he lived in a cave on St Michael's Mount, which is an island.

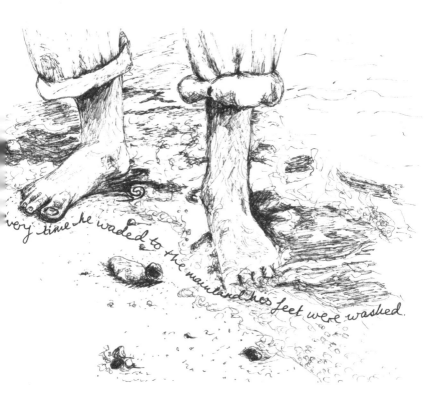

very time he waded to the mainland his feet were washed.

Every time he waded to the mainland his feet were washed, but he only had a bath when it was a very high tide.

As he waded out that morning he grumbled, as usual, as his feet were washed again. Crabs nibbled his shiny heels and eels slithered between his lovely clean toes.

Cormoran waded east, past the steep cliffs at Hoe Point, until he could see Pengersek Castle. Around it were green fields and there he would often steal a cow or two for breakfast. He never wondered why no one complained. In fact, he never wondered about anything much! But no one complained because at Pengersek Castle there was no one at home.

Lord Pengersek was away in the east, secretly learning to be a magician. After three years he passed all his magic exams, was given a big book of spells and a pointed hat, and was sent home to Cornwall. Next morning he got out of bed, opened the curtains, and was startled to see a giant picking up two of his cows and stuffing them into his trouser pockets. The giant was very big and rather smelly. Pengersek decided that confrontation would be neither wise nor pleasant: the giant was five times bigger than he was, even when wearing his wizard's hat.

It was clear to Pengersek that magic was the answer. He had never tried casting a spell on anything as big as a giant so he thought he would start with something simple.

In the field Cormoran was grumbling because the cows in his pockets were mooing loudly at the prospect of being eaten for breakfast.

The morning sun was shining on the giant's gleaming feet and Pengersek couldn't help but notice them. They gave him an idea. He looked in the book of spells for 'feet' and found the famous Sardinian wobbly feet spell. Pengersek recited the magic words. Cormoran found his feet behaving like buckets of jelly. He wobbled left, he wobbled right, and he looked very silly.

Encouraged by the success of his first spell Pengersek decided to move up the giant's legs. Having started with feet he then looked in the book for 'knees'. There he found the prize-winning Alpine bendy knee spell. Again he recited the magic words. Cormoran found his knees bending quite randomly. Sometimes he bent forwards; sometimes he bent backwards. He felt very silly indeed.

Now Pengersek was enjoying himself. He looked in the book for 'legs'. There he found the world-famous Cornish leg-control spell. For a third time he uttered the magic words. Suddenly Cormoran found himself not just wobbling backwards, forwards and sideways, but lurching across the countryside.

A big smile was now on Lord Pengersek's lips. By magic he steered Cormoran across the fields towards the sea. At first Cormoran didn't mind someone else being in charge of his legs. It was nice not to have the responsibility. But then he saw the sea getting closer and closer. To his dismay he realised he was being walked towards the cliff at Hoe Point. The giant struggled to stop or change direction, but nothing worked. Steadily he was wobbled to the edge of the cliff. He shouted for help, but there was no other giant for miles around. It seemed he was doomed.

At the edge of the cliff the giant closed his eyes tight and waited to fall into the sea.

Back at the castle Lord Pengersek was very pleased with his first three spells, but casting them was rather tiring, so he decided he would go to bed early. He had a light supper, put on his special magician's nightshirt and went to bed.

Out on the headland Cormoran nervously opened his eyes. In front of him was a huge drop into the sea. The water looked wet and cold and the rocks looked sharp. But now he could not move his legs at all. He watched the sun set. It started to rain; the wind blew. It was dark and cold. He tried sleeping standing up, but it didn't work because the cows in his pockets kept mooing and his wobbly knees were knocking with the cold.

The giant had never been so unhappy and tears welled up in his enormous eyes. At last, he saw the first light of dawn appear in the sky.

In his castle Lord Pengersek dressed by the warm fire and had a leisurely breakfast. He had steaming porridge, hot toast and marmalade, and warm tea. He was reading the morning paper when he was disturbed by a sad wailing sound, like a foghorn. He remembered Cormoran was still on the edge of the cliff.

The wizard put on his cloak to keep warm, pinned his wizard's badge prominently on the lapel and put on his pointed hat to look as imposing as possible. Even so he felt rather nervous, for although Cormoran was rooted to the spot he was still as tall as a church tower.

Luckily it had rained all night so Cormoran had been washed in cold water several times and was much less smelly than usual.

Pengersek tried to sound imposing, 'I am the great wizard Pengersek. My power is absolute. Why shouldn't I throw you into the sea?'

Cormoran wailed uncontrollably. At the wizard's command he took the cows from his pockets and put them on the ground, where they scampered happily away. He promised that he would never again steal anything. Then the wizard undid the spells and the giant walked sadly away.

Never again was Lord Pengersek troubled by any giant. Never again did Cormoran steal cows or sheep. And, do you know, there are still two cows who live in a field near Hoe Point, who tell their calves the story of the day when they went for a ride in a giant's pockets.

'Well told,' cried Anthony. 'My turn now.'

*(A book)*

# 30

## DEG WARN UGENS

## Marazion: Tom the Tinner

*A white stream:*
*My child is cream.*
*My bed is bread;*
*My son brings dreams.*

Tom the Tinner worked on the moors of West Penwith. He knew the secret places where streams cut into the granite and washed black tin-sand to the stream bed. In those days you could find beaches where the sand was black or striped, black and yellow, not because they were dirty, but because they were rich in tin washed down from the moors. Cornishmen wear shirts of those colours to this very day.

Tom used to pan for tin, swirling sand and water round a shallow bowl. The heavy, black tin ore would stay in the middle, and the light dust would wash over the side of the bowl. When Tom had gathered enough he would sell it at the market in Marazion, near the rocky island of St Michael's Mount.

Often on the way home he would visit his Aunt Nancy, who lived near Gulval. She was a farmer's wife. She kept chickens and cows, and always had lots of eggs, milk, butter and cheese.

Tom and Aunt Nancy would sit by the fire, drink mugs of tea, eat saffron buns, and tell each other stories. Then one day Aunt Nancy told Tom the story of the Giant of St Michael's Mount and his cave full of treasure.

So, the next time Tom went to Marazion market and sold his tin, as he sat on the shore gazing at the Mount, Tom thought, 'I wonder if the giant is still there?' He asked local people but no one knew. They were all too scared to find out.

If the tide is in you have to go to the Mount by boat, because it's too far to swim and too deep to wade, unless you happen to be a giant. But it was then low tide, when you can walk there on a stone causeway. So Tom set out for the Mount.

As he got near, Tom heard a low, rumbling noise. He guessed it must be the giant's breathing. Tom crept up to the cave. Several rats, ferrets and dogs ran out. Carefully he tiptoed inside, brushing away the cobwebs and spiders. Piled in the corners of the cave were gold and silver, jewels and all sorts of treasure.

But in the middle of the cave Tom saw a sorry sight. Cormoran was sitting on the side of his bed, sighing deeply. On the floor was a huge bucket to collect his tears and several small fish were swimming in it. The giant's feet were gleaming, but the rest of him was rather grubby. More importantly, the rest of him was very thin.

When Tom came in the giant wailed, 'Is that you, Wizard Pengersek?' Several tears splashed into the bucket, disturbing the fish.

'No,' said Tom. 'I'm Tom the Tinner, and I've come to see you.'

'You're not going to cast a spell on me are you?' trembled the giant. The fish hid at the far side of the bucket.

'No,' said Tom, 'I'm a tin streamer, not a magician. You look very thin; are you all right?'

'No,' said the giant. 'Since the wizard put spells on me I've been too scared to leave my cave and now I have nothing left to eat. I haven't had my croust* for weeks.'

'You poor giant,' said Tom. 'Don't worry, I will get help.'

Tom ran across the causeway and straight to Aunt Nancy's house. She filled a basket with eggs and butter and cheese. Tom carried a bucket of milk and they returned to the Mount. By now it was what Cornish fishermen call 'morlanow' or high tide, so a boatman rowed them out to the island. They clambered up the Mount, avoiding the rats, ferrets and dogs. They brushed aside the cobwebs and went into the cave. When Aunt Nancy saw the giant she was dismayed.

'You poor dear,' she cried, 'you'm half starved. Just give me five minutes and I'll make 'ee a cheese omelette. I 'ave the makings right here in my basket.'

Tom found a frying pan and started heating it on the fire. Then he put in the butter to warm. Aunt Nancy found a bowl and started mixing up the eggs with a drop of water and a pinch of salt and pepper. When the butter was foaming she poured the egg mixture into the frying pan. When it was nearly cooked she added the cheese and folded it in half.

Seconds later Cormoran was tucking into a huge cheese omelette, probably the largest ever made. He thought it was wonderful.

'Thank you,' he said, 'but I don't have proper money to pay you. Could I just give you some of this treasure lying in the corner of the cave? And please could you come back tomorrow and make me another omelette?'

So Aunt Nancy got the job of feeding the giant. He paid her in treasure, some of which she gave to Tom. Cormoran became the friendliest giant anyone had ever known, and they all lived happily ever after.

*(Milk)*

---

* croust – Cornish dialect for a snack or light meal.

# 31

# Prussia Cove: The King of Prussia

*I plough a many-acred field,*
*Where no seed ever grows.*
*Servant of the winds am I,*
*Master of the rose.*

They left Marazion before dawn and walked east across open heathland. Skylarks sang and so did Anthony. Cury was only a day away and he looked forward to being with his wife Martha and baby Sarah again. Then in the distance Jamie saw a hand-cart being hurriedly pushed across the road. It carried two large barrels and a chest. Suddenly two men sprang from the ditch, grabbed Anthony and Jamie, and dragged them into nearby trees.

'Dedh da,' said Anthony, quickly. The men looked surprised to be greeted in Cornish.

'Fatla genes?' asked one of them.

'Da,' replied Jamie, automatically.

'Marazion?' asked the other.

'Cury.' said Anthony. 'Nag o vy Sows.*'

'Even so, you've seen too much,' said the tallest man. 'You're for a swim.'

'He saw nothing,' said Jamie. 'He's blind.'

The men looked surprised. After a short argument they marched father and son down the lane towards the sea.

'We're taking you to the king,' they said.

After a mile they reached a low building.

'Into the Kiddly,' said the taller man.

Inside was the kindly landlady. 'Cheel, what brings you here?' she said to Jamie.

'Bessie,' said the tall man, 'they were on the turnpike at Rosudgeon when the lads were shifting the last load. But the old guy is blind.'

'Don''ee harm the cheel*,' said Bessie.

Anthony and Jamie were bundled through a door and down a rocky staircase to a sea cave. They were led onto a quay, then onto a ship.

Jamie whispered, 'It's the *Phoenix*; we saw it near Padstow.'

The ship's captain looked at him sternly.

Soon they were sailing out of the cove. Jamie saw cannon mounted on the cliffs above.

'Who are these people?' Jamie whispered.

'The Carters of Prussia Cove,' replied Anthony. 'Privateers and free traders: the wildest in the land, but honest too. The captain is John Carter: they call him the King of Prussia.'

The ship left the shelter of the land and heeled in the breeze. Jamie could hear the sailors spoke only Cornish. Then a look-out cried, 'Mirewgh dhe'n Orlewin! Gorhel an Myghtern*.'

Jamie saw a ship leaving Mount's Bay. A white ensign fluttered at its stern. The King of Prussia gave a command. The *Phoenix* turned south-east. Sailors hoisted a topsail and the ship raced along.

In an hour they reached Mullion harbour. Some crew fled among the cottages with small satchels. Others unloaded some barrels. Anthony and Jamie seemed forgotten. Jamie steered his father towards the gang plank.

'Come on Dad,' he said, 'we can escape.' Suddenly he felt a hand on his shoulder.

'Not so fast,' said the King of Prussia.

Jamie flinched but the King smiled. 'Let little children come to me, that's what it says in the Good Book. Off Padstow you and Tommy distracted that *Black Prince* just enough for me to catch him! I owe you a favour. Tell no one what you have seen or heard today. Go in peace,' he said. 'Dedh da.'

'Dedh da,' said Jamie as they stepped ashore.

*(A sailing ship – the rose is the compass rose)*

*Translation – 'good day', 'how are you?', 'good', 'I'm not English.'

* cheel – Cornish dialect meaning child.

* Translation – 'Look West! A King's ship.'

# ᴅᴇᴡᴅʜᴇᴋ ᴡᴀʀɴ ᴜɢᴇɴꜱ

# Cury: Every
# Summer a Song

*Four legs, four shoes,*
*A tale miles long.*
*A sky roof, an earth bed,*
*Every summer a song.*

As they walked to Cury Jamie rejoiced to see familiar landmarks: Poldhu Cove, with its fishing boats, then the tower of St Corantyn's Church. But when they reached their cottage the door was swinging open.

'Martha?' called Anthony.

Jamie rushed from room to room.

'Empty,' he cried.

Suddenly there was the sound of heavy boots. Redcoats appeared. A loud voice declared, 'You're under arrest!' Anthony and Jamie were dragged outside. A crowd had gathered. Jamie saw his mother and baby sister were held by soldiers, both were crying.

A tall figure appeared, it was Henry Boase, the magistrate. 'Got you!' he said. 'Funny isn't it. Wherever privateers are seen you're close by: Wadebridge, Port Quin, Padstow, Mousehole, Marazion, Mullion. What are you, Mr James, a smuggler or a spy? You travel freely; I think you are both. No, don't say anything, you talked your way out of my hands once before. It won't happen again. Do you have anyone to speak for you?'

Jamie could see only hostile strangers. It seemed hopeless. But then an old man fearlessly pushed through the crowd. It was Bill Chubb, all the way from Liskeard: 'I can tell you he's a storyteller. Nothing more, nothing less.'

Another figure stepped forward. 'So can I,' said Billy Hicks from Bodmin.

'So can I,' said Frosty Foss from St Just. 'Where's your proof, Mr Boase?'

Tommy the fisherman appeared: 'You are a fool fishing with no bait. Get ashore before the tide turns!'

Boase was about to arrest Tommy when he felt a hand on his shoulder. It was John Carter, the King of Prussia. Behind him was the entire crew of the *Phoenix*.

'Peace, Boase,' said Carter sternly, 'we are all subjects of the King. His justice requires evidence. Rumour and prejudice are not proof. All Cornwall knows Anthony James is a storyteller. His tales speak for him and for us too. His stories have brought us all here and what is happening now will be one of them. We all know the truth. Now you must tell us how this tale will end and how you will be remembered. We and the future await and expect your example.'

'Mr Carter,' said Henry Boase, 'rumour has it you are a scoundrel, yet I grant you are a wise man. In these troubled times my job is to pursue accusations, however unlikely. It is my job to be stern; I cannot tolerate fools.' Here he looked at Tommy. 'But you must tolerate me as I go about my business; it is that which keeps us all safe.'

Boase mounted his horse and rode away.

Then Anthony hugged Martha and baby Sarah, so did Jamie, and everyone joined in the biggest party there ever has been. Anthony and Jamie told everyone their adventures, so I wrote them in this book.

So it was then and so it is now. For every time there is a tune, every season a story, every summer a song.

*(Anthony and Jamie)*

in their heads was a world of stories, songs and tunes

## Society *for* Storytelling

Since 1993, the Society for Storytelling has championed the art of oral storytelling and the benefits it can provide – such as improving memory more than rote learning, promoting healing by stimulating the release of neuropeptides, or simply great entertainment! Storytellers, enthusiasts and academics support and are supported by this registered charity to ensure the art is nurtured and developed throughout the UK.

Many activities of the Society are available to all, such as locating storytellers on the Society website, taking part in our annual National Storytelling Week at the start of every February, purchasing our quarterly magazine *Storylines*, or attending our Annual Gathering – a chance to revel in engaging performances, inspiring workshops, and the company of like-minded people.

You can also become a member of the Society to support the work we do. In return, you receive free access to *Storylines*, discounted tickets to the Annual Gathering and other storytelling events, the opportunity to join our mentorship scheme for new storytellers, and more. Among our great deals for members is a 30% discount off titles in the *Folk Tales* series from The History Press website.

For more information, including how to join, please visit

www.sfs.org.uk